"I Want You In My Bed, Grace."

He trailed a path up her neck and along her jaw. "I want you wrapped up in nothing but me. I want to touch and feel every inch of your body with my hands and my mouth and tongue. I want to make you hot. I want to make you scream."

His mouth at her ear, his warm breath on her skin, made Grace feel boneless with the want rampaging through her.

So now the question was, did she trust Logan enough to allow him to do all those things his whispered promises had suggested?

Oh, who was she kidding? She wanted him so much, she could barely sit still. Heck, if she couldn't have trust, she would settle for lust.

* * *

To find out more about Harlequin Desire's upcoming books and to chat with authors and editors, become a fan of Harlequin Desire on Facebook, www.facebook.com/HarlequinDesire, or follow us on Twitter, www.twitter.com/desireeditors!

Dear Reader,

During the past year, I've introduced you to the three Duke brothers, Adam, Brandon and Cameron. Now it's time to meet their cousin Logan Sutherland. Logan and his identical twin brother, Aidan, spent their younger years surfing and swimming and partying, then won their first bar in a college poker game. Since that time, they've parlayed their winnings into a chain of lavish bars and resorts, plus an island or two. Logan Sutherland is wealthy, powerful and ambitious. (My favorite kind of hero!)

Enter Grace Farrell, a brilliant scientist who's lived her entire life inside a university laboratory, working on research that could save lives and change the world. Grace doesn't get out much, to say the least, but she's about to invade Logan's world in a major way!

Optimistic, scholarly Grace and cynical, worldly Logan couldn't be more different from each other. But to me, there's no notion more romantic than the concept of "Opposites Attract." It's going to take a lot to get these two diametrical opposites together, but they'll definitely find it's worth it in the end. It doesn't hurt that the story takes place on the Caribbean island of Alleria with its white sand beaches, tropical rain forest, hidden lagoons and turquoise waters. I can't think of a more beautiful setting for romance.

I hope you enjoy Logan and Grace's story! Please stop by my website, www.katecarlisle.com, and let me know. While there, you'll find pictures and links to some of the fantasy resorts I dreamed about while writing this story, as well as background stories and fun facts about me and my books.

Happy reading!

Kate

KATE CARLISLE

AN INNOCENT IN PARADISE

Recycling programs
for this product may
not exist in your area.

ISBN-13: 978-0-373-73142-8

AN INNOCENT IN PARADISE

www.Harlequin.com

Printed in U.S.A.

Books by Kate Carlisle

Harlequin Desire

How to Seduce a Billionaire #2104
An Innocent in Paradise #2129

Silhouette Desire

The Millionaire Meets His Match #2023
Sweet Surrender, Baby Surprise #2058

Other titles by this author available in ebook

KATE CARLISLE

New York Times bestselling author Kate Carlisle was born and raised by the beach in Southern California. After more than twenty years in television production, Kate turned to writing the types of mysteries and romance novels she always loved to read. She still lives by the beach in Southern California with her husband, and when they're not taking long walks in the sand or cooking or reading or painting or taking bookbinding classes or trying to learn a new language, they're traveling the world, visiting family and friends in the strangest places. Kate loves to hear from readers. Visit her website, www.katecarlisle.com.

To my four favorite plotters,
Susan Mallery, Maureen Child, Christine Rimmer and
Theresa Southwick. Thanks so much for the inspiration,
motivation, support, threats and laughs.
Drinks are on me, ladies!

One

Logan Sutherland was strolling toward the hotel lobby of the exclusive Alleria Resort when the jarring sound of shattering glass reverberated from the cocktail lounge.

"Price of doing business," Logan muttered. But he stopped and listened for another moment.

And heard nothing. Not a sound.

"Hell," he said, and checked his watch. The conference call was scheduled to start in fifteen minutes. He didn't have time for this. But the ominous silence made him change direction and head for the bar.

Logan and his twin brother, Aidan, had made their fortunes designing and operating exotic, upscale cocktail bars in high-end hotels all over the world. So the sound of breaking glassware was rarely a cause for alarm. But in his experience, the breakage was invariably followed by raucous cheers, jeers and laughter. Never silence.

Silence meant something was wrong. And Logan

Sutherland was not a man who allowed things to go wrong without doing something about it.

He walked into the casually elegant bar and noted that the sound level still hadn't risen, even though the place was busy and most of the tables were occupied by hotel guests having a good time. Cocktail waitresses and waiters moved swiftly from table to table, serving drinks and appetizers. The quiet was disconcerting.

A small group of his people were gathered in a knot at the far end of the long bar, all of them crouched on the floor. He approached the head bartender on duty. "What's going on, Sam?"

Sam flicked his chin toward the other end of the bar. "New cocktail waitress dropped a full tray of drinks."

"Why is it so quiet?"

Sam took a few seconds to study the drink station halfway down the long bar where two junior bartenders were efficiently refilling the drink orders. Then he turned and made eye contact with Logan. "We're all a little worried about her, boss."

"Why?" Logan glanced again at the small crowd. "Did she cut herself?"

He lifted a shoulder. "Naw, she's just a real sweet kid. It wouldn't be nice to laugh at her."

Logan frowned at the brawny former Marine, then turned to get a better look at the new employee.

The small group of servers and busboys picked up the last of the big chunks of broken glass and dispersed, heading back to their own stations. One waitress remained as a busboy swept the residual shards of glass into a dustpan. Then she knelt down and, with several bar towels, sopped up the rest of the liquid.

"Thank you so much, Paolo," the waitress said, and squeezed the busboy's arm affectionately. He took the clump of towels from her and she headed back to the drinks station. That's when Logan got his first look at the "real sweet kid." And felt a solid wall of heat almost knock him off his footing.

His *second* thought was: *Hope she's wearing sunblock,* because her skin was so pale and smooth and creamy.

His *first* thought had been vividly X-rated and not suitable for discussion in mixed company.

And none of that made him happy.

She was a classic redhead with a peaches-and-cream complexion and a light dusting of freckles across her nose. Thick, dark red hair tumbled down her back in rich, lustrous waves. In her official uniform of bikini top and filmy sarong, Logan couldn't help but notice she had a world-class butt and perfect breasts.

She was tall, a quality Logan preferred in his women—not that it mattered, since he didn't have time for or interest in a relationship right now. On the other hand, who said anything about a relationship? He could always make time for sex. Maybe he ought to rethink his schedule since staring at her was causing him to calculate how quickly it would take to get her into his bed.

She walked with the sort of poise that some tall women possessed naturally. That made the fact that she'd spilled a large tray of drinks even more baffling to him, since she didn't seem clumsy at all. On the contrary, she appeared confident and self-assured. Smart. Hard to believe she'd ever spilled anything in her life.

So what kind of game was she playing?

Logan thought of his tough bartender, Sam, calling her sweet and worrying about her sensitivities. Well, Sam wouldn't be the first man drawn in by a conniving, manipulative woman.

The woman in question finally noticed Logan and her

eyes lit up as she smiled directly at him. Okay, she was a stunner for sure. Logan felt as if he were the only man in the room and understood how his burly bartender had turned into such a pussycat in her presence.

Her mouth was wide and sexy, her lips full and lush. Her eyes were big and green and twinkled with an open friendliness that seemed genuine. She'd probably been practicing that generous smile forever. If nothing else, it would certainly help her garner the big tips.

Of course, she wouldn't be getting many tips if she kept spilling the customers' drinks. And that's why he was here, lest he forgot.

Before he could step up and introduce himself, the two bartenders finished her drink order and called her over.

"Oh, thank you, guys," she said, her voice as appealing as her smile. "You're both so sweet."

Logan watched the experienced bartenders' faces redden at the simple compliment, just as the woman pulled a small notebook from her waistband and studied it for a moment. She slipped the notebook away, then began arranging the drinks carefully on the tray in some kind of circular order. When she was finished, she grabbed the tray with both hands and started to lift it. There was a sudden hush around the room as the large tray bobbled awkwardly and the woman's eyes widened.

Without thinking, Logan rushed to her. He whisked the tray out of her hands, lifted it onto his shoulder and held it in place with one hand. Then he looked down at her. "Where's this going?"

"Oh, aren't you wonderful?" she said with another wide-eyed smile. "It goes right over here." She led the way to a four-top by the wall of windows overlooking the white-sand beach. She gestured with her hand. "These drinks are for Mr. and Mrs. McKee and their friends."

"Hey, doll," the older man said. "I told you I'd come and get those drinks for you, but it looks like you found yourself a helper there."

A guest of the Alleria resort was willing to get his own drinks for her? Okay, that was bad enough, but did this guest actually think Logan was the waitress's lackey? It was about time he and Ms. Clumsy had a long talk.

"Oh, Mr. McKee, thank you for offering," the waitress said, then turned and patted Logan's arm. "But all the servers here are so helpful that—"

"It's no problem at all, sir," Logan interrupted, lowering the drink tray onto the edge of the table. He quickly passed the drinks out, then said as affably as he could manage, "Enjoy your cocktails."

"You betcha, pal," Mr. McKee said and took a big sip of his banana daiquiri. "Man, these go down smooth."

"Here you go, sweetie," Mrs. McKee said, and tucked a fifty-dollar bill into the waitress's hand. "That's for all your trouble."

"Oh, my goodness," the waitress said, staring at the money, then back at her customers. "Thank you so much."

"No, thank *you,* doll." Mr. McKee winked. "You're a cutie-pie and we're just sorry we loaded you up with our orders."

She waved off the apology. "Oh, that's—"

"Thank you, Mr. and Mrs. McKee," Logan interrupted. "Please enjoy your day." Then he grabbed the waitress's arm and led her gently but firmly away from the table. He stopped at the bar, where he dropped off the tray, then scooted her across the room and out the door.

"Wait," she protested, squirming against him. "You have to let me go. I can't leave the lounge right now. I'm working."

"We're going to have a little talk first," Logan said,

smiling grimly as he led her down the hall toward his office.

"Stop," she insisted as she struggled to pull her arm from his grasp. "Honestly, who do you think you are?"

"At the moment I'm your employer," he said, glaring down at her. "But I don't expect that status to last much longer."

Grace cringed at his revelation. Of all the people to have rescued her from another spilled tray of drinks, why did it have to be one of the Sutherland brothers?

Before leaving for Alleria, Grace had done some cursory research on Logan and Aidan Sutherland. They'd risen to the top of the surfing world in their teenage years, then parlayed their winnings into fancy nightclubs and bars all over the world. Rumor had it they'd won their first bar in a college poker game; but Grace didn't believe that story was anything more than an urban legend.

The most recent story she'd read about the Sutherland twins centered on them joining forces with their cousins, the Duke brothers, who owned a number of luxurious resorts on the West Coast.

Grace had seen photographs of the Sutherland men online, but those pictures were all action shots of the brothers surfing or sailing. None of them had shown how good-looking they were up close, nor had the photos given her even one, tiny warning of the disconcerting amount of physical power and dynamism the man striding next to her would exude in person.

Halfway down the hall, her new boss stopped at a set of double doors and flicked a plastic card through a security slide. He ushered her through the door and into a large, beautifully furnished hotel suite. An attractive sofa and several overstuffed chairs in muted shades of chocolate-brown and rich taupe were clustered at one end of the large room. The other half of the room contained a set of large, elegant office furniture along with all the usual equipment necessary to run a twenty-first-century office.

"This is where you work?" She turned around slowly to take it all in. Plantation shutters were opened to reveal an entire wall of sliding glass doors that led to a wide private terrace and showed off the spectacular view beyond of palm trees, sunshine, pristine white sand and clear, turquoise water.

It was one of the most beautiful sights Grace had ever seen and she stopped to admire it for several long seconds.

"Nice view, isn't it?" Mr. Sutherland said.

"It's stunning," she said, and turned to look at him. "You're so lucky."

"Yeah, it's good to be king," he said, and flashed her a confident grin that made her knees go weak. She rubbed her stomach and wondered if maybe she should've had more to eat for breakfast than just granola and mango juice, because her knees had never gone weak before in her entire life.

But looking at him again, she realized she would just have to learn to live with rubbery knees. He was tall and imperious, she thought, with dark blue eyes that glimmered with cynicism. She hoped there was some glint of empathy underneath that cynicism.

He picked up the phone and when someone answered, he said, "Reschedule the conference call for four o'clock." Then he hung up and stared at Grace. She knew she was in trouble but it didn't stop her from enjoying the sight of those riveting blue eyes that seemed to see right through her. His jaw was firm and strong and he had a small cleft in his square chin. His nose was just slightly crooked, which gave him a raffish charm she found nonsensically alluring.

"Sit," he said brusquely, indicating one of the plush chairs that faced the massive mahogany desk. She sat quickly, then noticed that he'd chosen to remain standing. The better to intimidate her, of course.

But that was fine. If these were to be her last few minutes on the Caribbean island, she would be perfectly happy to spend them staring at Mr. Sutherland. The man was stunningly handsome and muscular—not that she'd seen any of his actual muscles in person. Sadly, his impeccably tailored black suit covered his rugged frame completely. But Grace knew the man was built because of the way he'd so casually taken that heavy drink tray from her hands and lifted it up onto his shoulder so effortlessly.

Granted, before this trip to Alleria she hadn't gotten out of her laboratory much, but she'd never seen anything quite like him. His arms and shoulder muscles had to be in remarkable condition. She itched to squeeze them.

And that was an absolutely ridiculous thought, she scolded herself.

"I'm going to go out on a limb here," he said, interrupting her pleasant daydream, "and bet that you've never worked as a cocktail waitress before. Am I right?"

She took a deep breath or two as she considered lying to him, then changed her mind. She'd never been very good at prevarication. Still, it wouldn't do to tell him everything. But then she argued with herself, Oh, why not? Finally she said, "Yes, you're right, but—"

"That's all I wanted to know," he said pleasantly. "You're fired."

"No!" she cried, gripping the arms of her chair. "You can't fire me. Not yet."

"Not yet?" he repeated. "Why not? Because you haven't had a chance to break my entire supply of glassware?"

Her shoulders sagged. "No, of course not. But…I can't go home."

His eyes focused in on her. "What's your name?"

"It's Grace. Grace Farrell."

"Wait a minute." He cocked his head as though he hadn't heard her correctly. "Your name is *Grace?*"

She nodded gravely. "That's right."

"You're kidding." He chuckled, then leaned his hip against his desk and began to laugh, a deep rich sound that caused tingles to stir in her stomach.

What the heck was so funny about her name?

"Oh," she said, finally getting the joke. The very *lame* joke, she might add. "Yes, well, I suppose I wasn't very graceful out there."

"You think?" He snorted.

She blinked and sat up straighter in her chair. "You don't have to be rude."

"Sweetheart, you're the one who lied on your job application."

"I didn't— How did you know I lied?" She groaned inwardly. She couldn't even lie about lying. That was just sad.

"Easy." He folded his arms across his impressive chest in a move Grace knew was meant to daunt her. And it was working, sort of. She was more than a bit overwhelmed by him, if her inability to breathe was any indication.

"I don't hire inexperienced waitresses," he continued. "Since we did hire you, your application must've stated that you knew what you were doing. And you obviously don't, which means you lied. And since you no longer work for me, I can be as rude as I want."

"I hope you'll reconsider," she said, sniffing with annoyance at the logic of his argument. "I had a very good reason for lying—er, fudging the truth."

"Fudging?" He leaned one hip against the edge of his desk. "I can't wait to hear this."

She frowned at him. "Are you willing to listen to reason?"

"I'm a reasonable man," he said, waving his hand at her as if granting her permission to speak. "Just make it fast. I was on my way to making a very important phone call when I was interrupted by your little scene out there."

"Oh, I'm really sorry about that."

"Yeah, me, too. So?"

"Right. Well, it's simple, really." She took a quick moment to wish she was dressed in something more professional than a bikini top that revealed most of her breasts and a thin wisp of cloth that was knotted well below her belly button. But since she couldn't exactly run back to her room and change clothes, she took another deep breath and blurted, "You have spores."

He stared at her for a length of time, then shook his head. "No, I don't. I bathe daily."

She blinked, gasped, then laughed. "Oh, no, not *you* personally. Your island. There are rare spores growing here on Alleria that will save lives someday. I'm a research scientist and I've come here to collect and study them."

He continued to stare her down as he seemed to consider the situation. She thought she saw something akin to a hint of reasoning in his eyes. But then he checked his watch and said, "Okay, nice try. I'll expect you off the island within the hour."

"What? No!" She jumped up from her chair. "Mr.

Sutherland, you don't understand. I refuse to leave this island. I need to stay here and work."

He shook his head. "I'm afraid you're the one who doesn't understand, Ms. Farrell."

"You're wrong. I do understand," she insisted, shaking her finger at him. "I know I lied and maybe you think you have every right to fire me, but I am not leaving this island until I get what I came for."

Logan couldn't help but admire the fire of righteous vehemence in Grace Farrell's eyes. It seemed to light up her entire body and made him wonder if she would show that same level of passion in bed. When he thrust himself into her, would she scream with pleasure?

His eyes narrowed at the mental picture and he shook himself back to reality. What the hell was he doing, thinking of her in terms of a sex partner? She'd lied on her résumé, broken his glassware and wasted his time. She had no business staying on his island a minute longer than necessary.

But the vivid sexual image took a few knots of wind out of his sails and he took a moment to reconsider the idea of throwing her off the island. Yes, she was a liar, but she was a gorgeous one. Why not enjoy a few rounds of mutually enjoyable sex before tossing her off the island?

Hell, that idea was growing more appealing by the minute. Maybe he'd been working too hard lately, because he realized he wasn't quite as ready to get rid of her as he was a few minutes ago. Didn't mean he trusted the woman for a second, but frankly, he hadn't been this amused or intrigued—or aroused—in months. That was worth a few minutes of his time. It wouldn't hurt to let her talk.

"So tell me about these spores you're so anxious to find," he said, as he sat and made himself comfortable on the overstuffed couch. Might as well enjoy the show for as long as it lasted, he thought.

She was pacing now and pounding her fist into her palm, clearly committed to her cause. "Allerian spores flawlessly mimic human reproductive genes and are essential to my continued experimentation in gene replication. I've been working on this project every day for almost ten years and have been using the same batch of spores for the past two years. It's imperative that I acquire a fresh consignment in order to obtain new funding and continue my studies."

"Gene replication?"

She stopped midpace. "You know what that is?"

"Well, sure." He frowned. "Generally. Yeah."

"Oh, that's good. That's wonderful!" She clasped her hands together and pressed them to her breastbone. "Then you understand how important my work is and how vital it is that I find new spores. My dissertation detailing their meiotic patterns and the ability to exploit the resulting haploid cells has already gained international interest. I'm positive that further study will ultimately lead to unlocking the secrets to curing some of the worst diseases known to modern man."

"Oh, yeah?" He'd lost her at "meiotic patterns" but wasn't about to mention it.

"Absolutely." She held up her thumb and forefinger and squeezed them together. "I'm this close to finishing the preliminary studies and I've applied for further grant money in order to move to the next level. It's urgent and important work. But I need fresh, large batches of spores and I need them soon."

"I see," he said, stretching his arm out across the back of the sofa.

Clearly frustrated by his blasé tone, she stopped her

pacing and said quietly, "Look, Mr. Sutherland, I am a scientist, a very good one. And I...I need this job here in order to conduct my studies. Your resort is the main source of employment on the island."

"It's the *only* source of employment, Ms. Farrell, but let's not nitpick." Staring out the sliding glass doors, he carefully avoided making eye contact as he returned to his original argument. "So the reason you lied on your résumé was so that I would hire you so that you could live here at my resort for free and study our spores."

"Well, yes, and—"

"And you thought you'd coast right into the mindless job of waitress in our cocktail bar to cover your costs."

"I suppose that's right, but—"

"And yet, you've never been a cocktail waitress."

"Well, no, but—"

"Well, then." He lifted his shoulders in a move meant to indicate only one conclusion. "At the risk of repeating myself, you're fired."

"Wait!" She rushed over and sat on the couch mere inches from him, her breasts rising and falling with her rapid, anxious breathing. Her scent, some exotic blend of spice and...was it orange blossoms?...enveloped him. Up close, he could see a pale smattering of freckles on her shoulders. He had the most bizarre urge to touch them.

"Haven't you heard a word I've said?" she said. "I'm not leaving."

"You don't have to leave," he said genially. "Feel free to book a room at the resort and study spores as much as you want. But don't expect me to subsidize your trip."

"But..." A heavy frown marred the smooth surface of her forehead and her lower lip was in danger of quivering. She wasn't going to cry, was she? If she did, Logan swore he would throw her out of here faster than she could say *meiotic*…whatever. Crying was the ultimate weapon of female manipulation. He'd learned that the hard way.

"I can't book a room here," she confessed. "It's too expensive. The only way I can stay is if you'll let me work for you."

He raised one eyebrow. "No."

"Fine," she said defiantly, and jumped up from the couch. "I'll sleep on the beach, but I'm not leaving."

"Wait just a damn minute," he said, standing. "Nobody sleeps on my beach."

She turned. "*Your* beach?"

"That's right. I own most of this island and I say who comes and goes. And I don't want vagrants setting up camp on my beach."

"I'm not a vagrant," she muttered as she folded her arms tightly across her chest. Her lower lip stuck out in a pout and as much as he hated the manipulation game, he had to admit he wanted to run his tongue over those pouty lips of hers. He had to give her points for that.

She swallowed nervously and took another deep breath and it seemed to help her regain some inner resolve. Her lips tightened and she faced him head-on. "I'm not leaving, Mr. Sutherland. I need to find those spores. I won't go home without them."

He observed her quietly for a long moment. "You don't look like a research scientist."

She rolled her eyes. "What do my looks have to do with anything?"

He almost laughed. Her looks had almost everything to do with why he'd allowed her to make her case in the first place. If she didn't understand that, then maybe she *had* been hiding out in a stuffy laboratory for the past ten years.

Wait. Ten years? He knew she couldn't be much older

than twenty-five, which meant she'd been doing her so-called research since she was fifteen. If she was telling the truth, that is. Obviously, she wasn't.

She was a liar, plain and simple.

Before he could comment aloud, she waved her arms and forged ahead. "Fine. I may not look like your notion of a research scientist, but that's exactly what I am. And I have every intention of staying here until I've got everything I need to finish my work."

"Is that right?"

"Yes."

He noticed she was barely able to keep from squirming under his sharp gaze. Good.

Then, without warning, she stepped even closer and stared hard at him, eye to eye. Well, eye to chest was more accurate, since he towered over her. But that detail didn't seem to intimidate her.

"Look, I'm not above begging," she admitted. "I intend to stay on this island and I'm willing to do anything you want me to do. If you refuse to let me be a cocktail waitress, I'll clean hotel rooms or wash dishes or…or water your plants. I just ask that my mornings be kept free for the spores. That's why the cocktail waitress job is ideal, but there must be something else I can do around here. Oh, I can cook! Well, I'm not a great cook, but I can make salads or cut up fruit or…"

Anything he wanted her to do? Did she realize how dangerous that offer was? Was she truly that naive? For a second or two, Logan wondered about her and her wide-eyed innocence, then roughly shook the thought away. He didn't believe it. Grace Farrell was as manipulative as every other woman he'd ever met. Intriguing, gorgeous, sexy, but a manipulative liar just the same.

Damn, his brain was fogging over from her erotic scent. Maybe he was crazy, but he wanted his hands on her.

"Fine," he said. "You've got one week to prove you can handle the cocktail waitress job. If not, you're off the island."

"Oh, thank you!" Without warning, she threw herself into his arms. "Thank you so much. I can do it."

He drew in her scent and warmth, then forced himself to take hold of her elbows and nudge her out of his arms. "Just make sure you don't break any more glasses."

"I won't, sir."

"And don't call me sir."

She smiled tentatively. "Mr. Sutherland."

"Nobody calls me that, either. It's Logan."

"Thank you, Logan. And please call me Grace." She surprised him by taking hold of his hand, then gazed up at him, unsmiling. "You have no idea what this means to me and to the world at large. And I promise, I'll be the best cocktail waitress you've ever hired."

"Oh, yeah?"

"Oh, yes," she said with confidence, then let go of his hand and whipped out her small notebook. "I'm very smart and a quick learner. I've already memorized the ingredients of every drink in the bartenders' guide I bought. And as far as lifting the trays? Well, it's just physics, after all. Simply a matter of determining the correct spatial placement of the glassware on the tray. Look."

She flipped the pages and showed him a diagram. "As you can see, it's an exact duplication of our own solar system. In miniature, of course. My theory is that if the drinks are dispersed in this pattern on the tray, equilibrium will be achieved and there shouldn't be any spillage."

His mouth twisted in an acerbic grin. "Interesting theory."

"Yes." She stared at the diagram, then back at him. "I was just a little surprised to find out how heavy the tray was when I lifted it. But I know I can—"

"That's right, Grace, it's more than just physics," he said deprecatingly. "There's also a little matter of balance and proper weight distribution, not to mention the right application of upper-body strength."

"Oh, that's good," Grace said, eagerly grabbing a pen from his desk to make some notes in her pad. "That's very good. So you agree, it's a perfectly simple job once you get the dynamics hammered down."

He shook his head and wondered when, exactly, he'd lost control of the conversation.

"Thank you so much, Mr. Sutherland." She slipped her notepad into her waistband, then gave his arm an encouraging squeeze. "I promise you won't be sorry."

"It's Logan," he repeated. "And you've got one week to improve or you're out."

Two

She'd escaped banishment by the skin of her teeth.

Shivering slightly at the recollection of yesterday's lecture from Mr. Sutherland, Grace continued folding and organizing her clothes in the sleek bureau drawer.

Despite the fact that she expected to be here at least a month, everything she'd brought barely filled two of the drawers. But, back in Minnesota, when she'd packed her suitcase, she'd figured she wouldn't need much more than a few shirts and shorts to wear while searching for spores during her off-hours. And the hotel provided a uniform for its cocktail waitresses.

"Uniform." She shook her head at the term. Serena, the lounge manager, had asked her size, then handed her two brightly patterned bikinis and a see-through scrap of cloth they laughingly called a skirt.

But Grace was desperate to stay, so she didn't really mind wearing the outfit. And she didn't mind carrying ten to fifteen pounds of drinks on her shoulders if it meant she could work and live in the hotel for a month while she collected her precious spores.

The fact that she only had a few days to prove she could carry those trays on her shoulders was something she didn't want to contemplate too closely. Needless to say, she'd begun an intense upper-body workout that morning, knowing she needed more strength in her arms and shoulders.

Glancing around the luxurious hotel room with its elegant white wainscoting, coffered ceilings and wide-open view of the sparkling Caribbean waters, Grace allowed herself to revel in a moment of happy amazement. How in the world had she landed in such a beautiful place?

Of course the question was rhetorical, she thought with a smile, since she knew exactly how she'd arrived.

But it was remarkable that less than forty-eight hours ago, she'd been racing through the Minneapolis airport to make her flight. It had been difficult to run in her wool coat and thick sweater, heavy jeans, gloves and boots.

What a difference between then and now. Today she wore a bright pink tank top, thin linen shorts and sandals.

The frantic energy she'd felt two days ago on her way out of town was still coursing through her veins. Even though she recognized the source of the energy, it was disconcerting all the same. She'd always lived a quiet, well-ordered, disciplined life. Predictable. Safe. But now she was flying blind with absolutely no idea of what would happen next. Logan Sutherland had made it more than clear that she was here on borrowed time.

She was annoyed that none of her research on the Alleria Resort had uncovered the fact that the Sutherland brothers actually owned most of the island. That little fact had taken her by surprise and Logan had known it and used it to his advantage. She would have to stay alert to any other revelations if she found herself in his company again.

As she brushed her long hair back into a ponytail, she took careful note of the fact that her neck and shoulders were warming up at the very thought of Mr. Sutherland. No surprise there. Despite his threats and ultimatums, he was the most wickedly attractive man Grace had ever seen.

Not that she'd seen all that many attractive men in her lifetime. She would've remembered. Her mind was a steel trap, after all. But, no, gorgeous men like Logan Sutherland didn't tend to hang around the university research laboratory much. More like, never.

She knew he'd expected her to cower when he'd issued his ultimatum. But Grace never cowered. She'd been challenged countless times in the past and had always risen to the occasion. Mr. Sutherland—Logan—had simply thrown down a different sort of gauntlet than she'd been faced with before.

No worries. Because what Logan hadn't taken into consideration was that Grace Farrell was nothing if not a fighter. She relished obstacles; the higher level of difficulty, the better. To her, this was a new game to play, a new puzzle to be solved. She would learn the rules of the game using logic and reasoning, just as she'd done throughout her life. Then she would decipher the puzzle and win the game. To do otherwise was inconceivable.

She glanced at the clock on the nightstand. It was time to go to work. But as she glanced out the picture window at the stunning views, she wished for just a moment that she could stop all the clocks, take all the time in the world and just enjoy herself. She wanted to feel the sun on her back, walk barefoot in the white sand and frolic in the blue waters of Alleria Bay. She wanted to drink champagne and kiss a handsome man under the Caribbean moon.

"Oh, don't be ridiculous," she admonished herself. Those kinds of thoughts were not only foolhardy, they were dangerous. The clock was ticking. Time was of the essence.

There was no place in her life for fun and frolic, never mind kissing. Her entire life, her research, everything she'd ever worked for, would go down the drain if she didn't act quickly to staunch the damage already done.

She checked her kit bag to make sure she had everything she needed, then grabbed a towel from the bathroom and left the hotel room.

Crossing the bright, tropical-themed lobby, Grace stepped outside and felt the first rays of the warm sun on her skin. She adjusted her sunglasses and walked a dozen yards along the rows of swaying palm trees until she reached the edge of the white sand beach.

Now this was paradise.

She allowed herself thirty seconds to breathe in the spectacular view of the tropical island. Startlingly clear water stretched as far as the eye could see. Behind her, farther inland, were rolling green hills studded with more palm trees and lush vegetation. Sailboats bobbed at their moorings in the bay and sea birds flew overhead.

Her thirty seconds were up. Taking another deep breath, she hunkered down for the next forty minutes. Walking from palm tree to palm tree, she searched the base of each trunk where the roots divided, looking for a sign of the rare Allerian spores she'd come here to observe.

The sun was already warm at eight o'clock in the morning and she was glad she'd doused herself in sunblock. She should've brought a hat with her, too; but she'd been in such a hurry to pack and leave Minnesota that she hadn't fully considered the effects of the tropical sun on her sensitive skin. At times like this, she was forced to admit she wasn't quite as smart as everyone thought she was.

Another case in point, her awkward conversation with Logan Sutherland yesterday. She cringed inwardly, knowing that most of what he'd accused her of was true. Yes, she'd lied on her résumé, although that was for a good cause. But what she really hated admitting was that she'd foolishly underestimated the job of cocktail waitress. That wasn't smart. She wouldn't make that mistake again, especially after seeing firsthand how hard everyone in the bar worked.

"Just let that go," she murmured. At least Logan had relented and allowed her to stay, thank goodness. She had a full week to redeem herself and she vowed to do just that, if only for the sake of the spores.

Now if she could only find the darling little critters.

A sailboat under full sail skimmed across the bay and Grace stopped to watch it. Everywhere she turned on this island, in any direction, she could find something new and wonderful and exotic to look at. She stretched and allowed the sunshine to permeate her skin. Had she ever felt this warm and cozy without the benefit of a down jacket?

She'd lived in Minnesota her entire life and she was perfectly happy there, of course. But she was just beginning to realize that she'd spent a good portion of her life being cold. No, not just *cold,* she thought. *Chilled to the bone.* She was so tired of being cold, so weary of bundling up in heavy coats and mittens and long underwear and wool scarves for more than half the year.

Alleria was beautiful and, more important, it was *warm.* If she couldn't truly let herself go and relax and enjoy her time here, she could at least savor the warm weather. It was so completely different from anything she'd ever experienced before.

Standing in a cozy patch of shade cast by a huge cluster of coconuts hanging in a nearby palm, Grace took another minute to stretch out her muscles. She rolled her shoulders and raised her arms up in the air, then bent at the waist to touch her toes. She was starting to ache a little from her upper-body workout and it felt good to stretch and bend.

Once Logan had pointed out the need for balance and upper-body strength, Grace had known what she had to do. She'd begun with thirty push-ups when she first got out of bed this morning. She was in decent condition physically, but she needed much more strength in her upper arms if she expected to lift those hefty cocktail trays every night.

She was determined to make Logan Sutherland acknowledge that she took her waitressing job seriously. She couldn't afford to be sent home. She absolutely had to get her funding; and to do that, she had to find and collect enough Allerian spore specimens to conduct her lifesaving experiments for the next few years.

As she straightened up and moved to another tree, she pondered the sadly obvious fact that Logan Sutherland couldn't care less about her scientific work. No, he just cared that she performed her job as cocktail waitress as well as anyone else in the company. But if that's what it took to keep her here, that's what she would to do.

At each coconut palm tree, she knelt down and examined the juncture where the thick palm roots crisscrossed and divided. Feathery fern leaves sprouted here and there and that was where her spores were known to propagate. But tree after tree, frond after frond offered exactly nothing.

She wandered away from the shore and deeper into what looked like a jungle of wild plants and palm trees. Here the thicker vegetation created more shade, but instead of being cooler, it was warmer and muggier. The overabundance of plant life kept the sea breezes from filtering through and cooling the air. Humidity was a good thing if you were a spore.

Sure enough, minutes later in a shady cluster of coco palms, surrounded by the soft fern leaves that protected them, Grace finally came across the spores she'd traveled thousands of miles to find.

"Ah," she whispered, "there you are, my lovelies."

She spread the clean towel on the sand and unzipped her spore kit. Kneeling on a corner of the towel, she used her most powerful magnifying glass to study the precious plant life more closely.

Unlike many plants, these types of spores could thrive without sunlight, but they still needed a warm, moist environment. Glancing around, Grace saw that this part of the island was indeed ideal. The sun was only beginning to shine here so the spores had a part of the morning to thrive in the muggy shade. They seemed happy, reproducing madly even as she watched them through the ultramagnified glass.

Grace smiled at the thought of happy spores. A sense of calm came over her as she observed the microscopic world. She had been experimenting on this rare strain of Allerian spores for so many years, ever since old Professor Hutchins, her teacher and first mentor, showed her his excellent treatise based on the first spores he brought back from the island. That dissertation had led Grace to begin her own experiments using the potential lifesaving properties of these little guys.

Grace glanced up at the clear blue sky and marveled at how far she'd come in her studies of the Allerian spores. They were valuable for so many reasons, including the gene replication studies she'd mentioned to Logan. But she was even more excited by the fact that the mitochondria

found within the spore cells contained a rare type of phy-
tohormone that carried potential medical applications. Her
latest experiments had proven that these hormones could
have an adverse effect on human cancer cells, causing certain cells to be suppressed or, in the case of her most recent
lab trials, to die altogether.

The possibility that Grace's studies could lead to the
destruction of cancer cells thrilled her as nothing else had
before. She could no more stop this important research
than she could stop breathing.

She thought back to the day she first walked into the
university laboratory when she was eight years old. She'd
spent hundreds of lonely hours in the lab since then, but
knowing that all those years of research might ultimately
lead to so many lives being saved made her forget her own
pain. It had all been worth it.

Recently, Grace had entered a new and critical phase
of her research. And even though some of the Professor's
last batch of spores were still producing decent progeny,
they were beginning to die out. Grace required a fresher,
stronger crop of the rare organisms to meet her current
needs.

"Current needs," she grumbled, shaking her head in
disgust. If it weren't for Walter Erskine trying to steal her
entire life's work, including taking credit for her latest experiments and proven theorems, she wouldn't be so desperate right now. Her cheeks still burned as she recalled how
easily Walter had charmed her, how quickly she'd grown
to like him, how fervently she'd hoped they would be together always. And she'd actually believed he reciprocated
her feelings. Could she honestly have been that naive?

She shook herself free of those unhappy thoughts. She
refused to blame herself for falling for his lies. Walter had
been quite the smooth operator, after all. Almost everyone

in the department had been fooled. But it was *Grace's* job that was on the line now, not anyone else's.

Snapping on a pair of disposable gloves, she pulled out one of her sterilized petri dishes. With her forceps, she carefully plucked a thick clump of spores from the fibrous base of the frond and held it over the dish. After tapping the forceps against the side of the dish, she watched the spores drop into the dish along with bits of moss and sand.

For the next hour, she repeated the process several more times. She numbered each petri dish and noted in her book the location and features of the palm tree, the angle of the sun and the temperature at the precise time she gathered each of the groups of spores.

Her stomach growled and she realized she was famished. Earlier, she'd eaten breakfast with other members of the hotel staff in their private cafeteria. Everyone was so nice to her and she'd felt almost decadent as she chose the colorful fruit platter with its dollop of yogurt. She hadn't seen such gorgeous fruit in Minnesota in a long time, if ever. But now, as she worked under the hot sun, she felt a little dizzy and determined that she would need to eat a bigger breakfast each morning. The last thing she wanted to do was pass out on the beach. She could only imagine what Logan Sutherland would say about that.

Checking the dishes stacked in her kit bag, she decided she had enough spores from this particular tree. It was a good start. She pulled off the gloves, packed up her kit and pushed herself up off the ground, anxious to return to her room where her microscope and portable lab equipment waited for her.

"Wow," she said with a laugh, as she brushed the fine grains of sand off her legs. "Do you know how to have a good time or what?"

She turned and almost collided with Logan Sutherland, who grabbed hold of her shoulders to steady her.

"What are you doing out here without a hat on?" he demanded, glaring at her.

She'd been so absorbed in her work that she hadn't heard him approach, but she should've sensed his forceful presence. He wore cargo shorts with a faded Hawaiian shirt and waterproof sandals. His skin was tanned a deep bronze and there was a hint of beard stubble on his jaw. He was laid-back and casual, so why did he look even more dangerous today than he had in his thousand-dollar suit yesterday?

She realized that the sun had shifted and she was now standing in bright sunlight. "I've been in the shade most of the time," she said lamely.

"You'll soon find out that doesn't make much difference this close to the equator." He took his baseball cap off and handed it to her. "Here, wear this. It's not much, but it'll protect your face for a while."

"It's not necessary," she said, taking a step back from him. He was so big and masculine, it was a bit overwhelming so early in the morning. And it was unnerving to realize that he was studying her as carefully as she would examine a particularly fascinating germ under her microscope. Maybe that's why she felt so shaky. "I'm going back to my room right now."

"Ten minutes out here is enough to make a difference. Put the damn hat on."

"All right." He was pushy, but he probably knew what he was talking about. Besides, she didn't want to give him any reason to think her uncooperative. She slipped her ponytail through the strap in back and adjusted the cap on her head. "Thank you. I'll get it back to you this afternoon."

"No hurry," he said. "We've got a gift shop filled with

wide-brimmed hats. You'll need one if you're planning to work outside every morning."

With a nod, she said, "I'll be sure to buy one this afternoon."

"Good. And buy more sunblock," he added brusquely. "I'd hate to see your skin get burned."

"Thank you." *I think,* she added under her breath, since he sounded almost angry about it. But she decided not to blame him. He'd probably seen his share of hapless tourists suffering from second-degree sunburns.

He stuck his hands in his pockets. "So you've been out looking for spores?"

"Yes. I've found a thriving colony right here," she exclaimed, energized all over again. Kneeling back down at the base of the palm tree, she pulled out her magnifying glass and handed it to him. "Come and see."

"Spore porn?" he said dryly. "I can't wait."

She smiled at him. "I'm sure you think it's odd, but I actually find it quite fascinating to watch them reproduce."

He knelt down next to her, so close that their shoulders and hips were touching. Taking the glass from her, he bent down and stared for a while. Then he straightened and gazed at her. "So they're basically having sex right now?"

Her eyes widened. His face was a mere inch away from hers. If he leaned in... But he wouldn't, of course. What was she thinking? She took a moment to swallow around her suddenly dry throat. "Um, yes. I suppose you could call it that. They do it around this time every morning."

One eyebrow shot up. "I guess you've got to admire their discipline."

"Oh, I do, I do," she murmured, mesmerized by his flirtatious smile. He had beautiful, straight, white teeth and his mouth had a sexy, sardonic curve to it that she found nearly irresistible. Oh, my, she thought. Was he moving closer to her? He stared into her eyes, then his gaze shifted to her lips. Was he going to kiss her? She could feel herself melting. She really should've worn a hat.

Standing abruptly, she said, "I've got to go. Got to get these back to the room. Got to… Well, goodbye."

She took off like a startled bunny and could actually feel his gaze locked on her as she ran down the beach. On her mad dash back to the hotel, she berated herself for behaving so foolishly. Had her emotions shown on her face when she realized his mouth was a few millimeters away from hers? She hoped not, but she knew she wasn't sophisticated enough to fake a look of bland disinterest in a moment like that.

Despite knowing he wanted her off the island, despite knowing he would use any excuse to get rid of her, she still found him irresistible.

"But you will resist him," she said sternly. She had no choice. She might've spent the past fifteen years working in near isolation in the university biogenetics laboratory, but she hadn't been completely cut off from real life. She read books and magazines; she socialized somewhat, if you could call it socializing when her current mentor—who was also her closest friend—invited her over once a month to have dinner with her big, boisterous family. Grace was grateful for those invitations since she was rarely invited to spend time with her own odd family.

The point was, Grace was savvy enough to know that where a man like Logan Sutherland was concerned, she was in way over her head.

From now on, she would keep her distance from her fine-looking boss. She would be polite and do what she had to do to impress him in the cocktail bar. But, outside of work, she would avoid him, evade him, do anything she had to do to stay away from him. She couldn't forget that he wanted her gone, off the island and away from the spores that were critical to her life's work.

And yet, dealing with Logan Sutherland would be a piece of cake compared to the hell she'd lived through the past six months. All she had to do was remember the bottom line: she wasn't leaving this island until she was damn good and ready to.

Three

The cocktail lounge was packed with happy people drinking, laughing and dancing. The music was mellow jazz, just loud enough to enjoy but not so overbearing that people had to shout to be heard. The lighting was subtle enough to make everyone look good and was embellished this evening by the glow of a full moon reflecting off the dark blue waters of the bay.

Logan had a dozen other things he could've been doing tonight. He usually made a point of stopping by the bar most evenings to say hello to guests and lend his presence in the rare instance that someone was causing trouble. But he didn't usually linger for long. He and his brother had hired the best, most trustworthy and well-trained employees, who knew the service business inside and out. They didn't need Logan hanging around, standing sentinel like an overanxious mother hen, driving his bartenders and staff crazy. Or worse yet, making them think Logan had no confidence in them.

But he was here anyway—and he wasn't leaving. He attempted to look casual as he leaned his elbow on the bar and sipped his thirty-year-old single-malt scotch. He let the smooth liquid heat its way down his throat and tried like hell to pretend he wasn't here to keep an eagle eye on his newest employee.

"Order up, Grace," Joey, one of the bartenders, called.

"Thanks, Joey," Grace said, rewarding him with a generous smile as she placed one of the wide trays on the bar and began to load it with drinks.

Logan noted that, as promised, she hadn't spilled a drink tonight. But that was only because her customers and the other waiters had been so willing to step in and help her carry her trays. One guest had even bussed a few tables for her. It was the strangest thing Logan had ever seen.

Usually, his waitstaff were territorial about their customers and tips. But with Grace, they all chipped in and helped her. Logan grudgingly admitted it was to her credit that she was quick to split her generous tips with all of them.

She loaded the drinks onto a large tray in that spiral pattern she'd insisted was cosmologically sound. Logan had to shake his head at that cockamamy theory, but sobered as he watched her shoulders tense up. She licked her lips and tested the tray's weight. Was she really going to try to carry it? There had to be at least ten drinks on the tray. What was Joey thinking?

Logan pushed off from the bar and moved toward her. But before he could get close enough to grab the tray, Clive, a witty Englishman and one of his top waiters, slipped smoothly behind Grace and rested his hands on her hips.

"Brace your knees, love," Clive said, "and put all your strength right here." With that, he skimmed the edges of her slender thighs all the way down to her knees. Then he moved around to face her and patted his own stomach. "Breathe from here. Muscles nice and tight."

Logan froze in place, his teeth clenched, determined not to step in and save her again. Instead, he would allow Clive to instruct her, unless it started to look like she would need more skilled intervention from Logan himself.

He watched Grace's breasts move in rhythm with the deep, anticipatory breaths she took. Then she was flying solo, following Clive's instructions, steadying her legs and lifting the tray onto her shoulder.

Clive and several other waiters watched with apprehension as Grace moved slowly across the room to a table of guests sitting near the window. Bending her knees, she set the tray down on the table. Half the staff applauded and Logan's tight jaw relaxed.

Grace's face lit up as she glanced around at her odd group of supporters. When her gaze met Logan's, her happy smile faltered.

Hell. He hated to be the cause of her bright eyes dimming, so he quickly grinned at her and flashed a thumbs-up sign. Her eyes widened and, as her smile grew, the entire room seemed to light up, as well.

Satisfied that she was happy and would survive the night, Logan turned back to the bar and took a last sip of his drink. But before he could even swallow, reality smacked him upside the head and he noted with disgust that she'd manipulated him again. Who cared if she smiled, for God's sake? She wasn't here to be happy. She was here to earn her paycheck or go home, damn it.

Waving down the head bartender, he snarled out his order, "Pour me another scotch, Sam."

Taking advantage of the early-morning quiet, Logan hauled his windsurfing board down to the deserted beach just as the sun was cresting over Alleria Peak. He slipped the board into the water, adjusted the mast and sail and then slid on top and started paddling.

It might've sounded strange to someone who didn't know him, but from the first time he swam in these waters, Logan had recognized Alleria as home. It was warm all year round so he never had to wear a wet suit. And it was clean. Even at twenty feet, he could see the sandy bottom of the sea. That was a minor miracle after years of surfing and sailing the rough and churning waves off the coast of Northern California—where he and his brother had grown up and where, when they were seven years old, their father had taught them how to surf.

Logan paddled a few more yards out. Then in one quick move, he rose to a standing position on the board and yanked the uphaul rope, pulling until the sail was upright. Grabbing hold of the mast and boom, he angled the sail until it caught the barest hint of wind. Balancing his weight on the board, he turned and headed for open water beyond the tip of the peninsula that formed the bay.

Alleria Bay itself was a tranquil inlet with few waves and the mildest of winds. But out beyond the break, the eastern trade winds provided plenty of excitement for any resort guests interested in windsurfing or sailing.

In a few hours, Logan would have contracts to study and phone calls to make. But right now, surrounded by wind, water and speed, he tried to blow off all thoughts of business and enjoy the moment. It wasn't easy; he was hardwired for success and had had a difficult time relaxing lately.

An unexpected swell crested and broke into a wave inches from his board. Logan took instant advantage, raking the sail back, then throwing the mast hard into the wind while jumping and lifting the board into the air and twirling it over the wave.

"Hot damn," he shouted with good humor. He'd managed a one-hundred-eighty-degree flaka, a hotdog maneuver he hadn't pulled off in years. He laughed as the wind picked up. The move reminded him of the days when he and Aidan had lived to surf. Back then, Logan had considered surfing the closest he would ever get to spirituality. It was all wrapped up in the notion of man and nature coming together through the elemental forces of the universe, the movement of water against earth, the changing of the tide, the passing of time.

He could still recall that exact moment in his youth when he'd stared into the eye of a twelve-foot wave and realized that if he could stand up on a flimsy piece of fiberglass and ride over the spuming water like Poseidon on a dolphin-teamed chariot, he could damn well conquer anything.

That understanding had kept both brothers at the top of their game as they traveled the world and competed in—and won—numerous international competitions. Because they were identical twins competing at the highest echelon of surfing circles, they were often treated like celebrities with all the perks that came with the territory. Especially women. They were everywhere and temptation was strong.

It was a wild life that might've eaten them up if they hadn't taken to heart the life lessons their father had taught them early on. Thanks to Dad's good example, they didn't take the lure of the high life too seriously. They also followed the number-one rule of surfers everywhere: *Never turn your back on the ocean.*

In other words, Logan thought: *Pay attention.* A guy never knew when a wave might knock him down or a shark would eat him alive.

Logan had learned the hard way that the rule applied to women especially. He'd let down his guard five years ago when he met Tanya and convinced himself he was in love with her. When he asked her to marry him and she said yes, he thought his life was complete. A year into their marriage, she was killed in a car crash and he thought he might die along with her. It wasn't until the funeral that Logan found out she had been driving off to meet her lover, some clown that had worked in the twin brothers' accounting office.

Never turn your back on the ocean. If his wife's betrayal wasn't enough to remind him that women, like sharks, were not to be trusted, Logan only had to remind himself that his own mother had deserted them when he and Aiden were seven years old.

With a determined pull on the boom, Logan angled the sail around and headed back to land. For the past few years, his emotions had drifted between grief that Tanya had to die and guilt that he'd never really loved her anyway. He had finally resigned himself to the fact that he just wasn't capable of love—and that was fine with him. Women were in plentiful supply and he certainly enjoyed them. A lot. The more the merrier. But that didn't mean he would ever fall in love and he sure as hell would never trust another woman again.

As he sailed closer to the beach, he spotted Grace Farrell walking through the clusters of palms growing in profusion along the bay. The muscles of his hands tightened around the mast and boom as he watched the gorgeous research scientist pause at each palm tree to study the roots and base. He was glad to see she'd taken his advice and worn a wide-brimmed hat today, along with a loose shirt with sleeves that would protect her sensitive shoulders from the unrelenting heat of the sun.

But there was barely anything covering up her long, shapely legs and even from this distance, he could appreciate the view of those legs and her luscious bottom as she bent over to search for spores.

Spores, for God's sake.

After a moment, she straightened up, then noticed him and waved. He grinned and aimed the board in her direction and sailed to within a few feet of the beach.

"Good morning," she said.

"Same to you." Logan folded the rigging and secured it to the board with a Velcro strap. Then he pulled the board onto the sand far enough to insure that it wouldn't slip back into the water.

"Hunting for more spores?" he asked.

"Yes," she said. "Have you been out long?"

"About an hour," he said.

She stared at the board, then back at him. "How in the world do you stay upright on that thing?"

Logan ran both hands through his wet hair, pushing it back from his forehead. "It's magic."

"It would have to be," she mused. Her gaze slipped down to his wet, bare chest. "Would you like my towel?"

"No, thanks. I'm okay."

She held it out for him. "But you're so wet and, um, well, it's your towel, actually, since I took it from my hotel room."

"Well, since it's mine," he said, chuckling as he took the towel. Maybe she hadn't seen many dripping-wet men in swim trunks back at her research lab because she seemed

awfully flustered. He hoped like hell that he made her un-
comfortable. It would serve her right for manipulating and
lying to him.

He took his time drying himself off as he studied her.
She'd been on the island four days now and true to her
word, she spent each morning hunting for spores, then
worked the cocktail lounge in the afternoons and evenings.
And she hadn't dropped a single glass since the first day's
fiasco.

He noticed her cheeks had a rosy pink glow from her
mornings in the sun. He liked the glow almost as much
as he liked her fabulous legs and perfect rear end. Even
knowing the woman was a liar and not to be trusted,
Logan found her incredibly appealing. He wanted her in
his bed with an urgency that was going to reveal itself any
second now if he didn't get the hell out of here.

"I've got work to do," he muttered finally, and handed
her the towel as he walked away.

Grace clutched the damp towel as she stared at Logan's backside until he disappeared through a door into
the hotel. Then she pressed the towel to her face to cool
herself off. She was certain she'd never met such a formi-
dable man. Certainly not one with a body like that. Or eyes
like that. Or hair, so adorably short and blond and spiky
when wet.

But for goodness' sake, did that mean she had to practically drool in front of him? And could she possibly have
thought of anything dumber to say to him? *How in the
world do you stay upright on that thing?* What was wrong
with her?

She blamed it on his smile. This was the first time he'd
smiled at her without showing his sarcastic or ironic side.
The sweetness of it had nearly blinded her. And talk about

upper-body strength. The man was built. She'd wondered what he looked like under his business suit and now she knew. The knowledge was life affirming, to say the least.

She turned back to her task but was still trying to shake off the effects of Logan's smile ten minutes later. She silently recited the periodic table of elements, an effective trick she used whenever she was having trouble concentrating. Unfortunately, it wasn't working today. She feared that smile of his might have a half-life of more than several hours because she was still caught up in its spell.

With a sigh, she walked away from the beach and deeper into the forest of vegetation. Despite the heat, she appreciated the extra layer of humidity, knowing it was the best breeding ground for her beloved spores.

"Beloved spores," she uttered aloud, shaking her head. Did that sound pathetic or what? But the truth was, sometimes she felt closer to the tiny, one-celled meiotic organisms than she did to people. Well, except for Phillippa, of course. Her lab partner and mentor had been her friend for years and right now, she could use someone to talk to. One thing she loved about Phillippa was that she always had an opinion about everything. Grace wondered what her friend would think of Logan Sutherland.

Grace was certain Phillippa would declare him "hawt."

Okay, he was hot, all right. But as she pushed past a giant fern, Grace gave herself a good talking-to. It didn't matter whether Logan was hot or not. He was her boss and Grace had no business thinking of him that way. All she needed from Logan Sutherland was his approval of her work in the cocktail lounge, nothing more.

She forced all thoughts of Logan away and got to work, backtracking to the palm trees where she'd found spores yesterday. Close to the base of each tree, she pounded a discreet wooden marker into the sand so she would know the trees from which she'd already extracted specimens. She planned to remove the stakes on her last day here; but, until then, they would provide a handy map for her to follow.

An hour later, she left the palm trees behind and headed back to the hotel. After running into the staff commissary to grab a sandwich, she returned to her room to document her findings and refrigerate several more petri dishes filled with fresh specimens. She showered and dressed for work, happy she'd been assigned to the swing shift from two o'clock to ten. The bar stayed open until three in the morning and the servers on the late shift got the best tips, but Grace preferred to wake up early and go to bed relatively early.

As she walked through the lobby toward the cocktail lounge, she passed a pretty young woman sitting on one of the smooth rocks that surrounded the tropical waterfall, crying. Grace paused, wondering if she should say something. Would the management frown on a cocktail waitress approaching a hotel guest? Did it matter? The woman was clearly distressed, so Grace went with her instincts and walked over to the woman.

"Are you all right?" she asked.

The woman looked up and pressed her lips together to stop from blubbering in front of a stranger. "I'm fine."

"We both know that's not true." Grace sat next to her. "Is there anything I can do for you?"

Fresh tears dripped down her cheeks. "I'm on my honeymoon."

"Then you should be happy, not sad," Grace said.

"But…I can't talk about it."

"Sure you can." Grace patted her knee. "I'm not sure I can help, but I can certainly listen."

* * *

Logan halted halfway across the lobby when he spotted Grace deep in conversation with one of the hotel guests. They sat by the tropical waterfall and he approached cautiously, not wanting to make a scene. But caution wasn't necessary. The women were so engrossed in their chat, they didn't notice him.

Grace was dressed for work in her bikini top and sarong, and Logan knew without checking his watch that her shift was about to begin. So what was she doing out here? He stepped closer.

"So if he spends more time right here at this spot," Grace said, tapping her notepad with her pen, "I think you'll be very happy."

The young woman took Grace's notepad and stared at some diagram she'd drawn. "Are you sure it's right there? He didn't seem to get anywhere near that spot."

"But he will," Grace said. She took the notepad, tore out the page with the diagram and handed it to the woman. "It'll make a big difference, I promise."

"I hope so," the woman said with a watery smile. "I don't want to spend my entire honeymoon crying."

"I'm sure your husband doesn't want that, either."

The woman hugged Grace, then jumped up. "You're so smart. Thank you."

Grace looked at her wristwatch and stood. "Please let me know how it goes. I work in the cocktail lounge in the evening or you can find me on the beach most mornings."

"I will." She waved the piece of paper as she hurried away.

Grace waved, then turned toward the cocktail lounge— and gasped. "What are you doing here?"

"I own the place," Logan said, folding his arms across his chest. "What was that all about?"

She fluttered her hands in the air. "Oh, nothing. Sorry I can't talk now. I have to get to work."

"It's okay. I know the boss." He grabbed hold of her arm. "You can be a few minutes late. Now tell me what's wrong with that woman. Did someone from the hotel bother her?"

"From the hotel? Oh, no. Absolutely not."

"You sure?"

"Yes, I swear it. She just had a...a little disagreement with her new husband. I saw her crying and I tried to comfort her."

"That's it?" Logan glanced in the direction the woman had gone, then back at Grace. "Is she all right?"

"I think she'll be fine," Grace said.

"Good," he murmured. "That's good. I don't like to see my guests crying in the lobby."

She nodded earnestly. "I can see how that would be a problem. But she's okay, I promise. Now I'd better get to work."

"Fine." Logan watched her walk all the way across the lobby and into the lounge. No doubt about it, the woman had a world-class backside and he itched to get his hands on her. He wasn't particularly happy about it because she was basically a pain in his neck. But as he walked back to his office, he resolved to seduce her as soon as possible. And then he'd kick her off his island.

"Six piña coladas, Joey," Grace said, and wished she could sit down and rub her feet. Anyone who ever thought waitressing was an easy job should be forced to do it for a week wearing high heels.

"Coming up, Gracie girl," Joey said.

She smiled at her coworkers' nickname for her. Nobody had ever called her Gracie until she arrived in Alleria. She liked it. She'd never thought much about it before, but back home, everyone took her so seriously. A few people called her Grace, but usually she was addressed as Doctor Farrell. Even by her parents, who were completely intimidated by her title and her intelligence. Nobody here called her Doctor Farrell, thank goodness. They had no idea she had four PhD's and would probably laugh their butts off if they found out.

"Hunk alert at three o'clock," said Dee, a pretty, dark-haired waitress from New Jersey, as she sidled up next to Grace.

Grace glanced at her watch. "What happens at three o'clock?"

Joey and Dee exchanged grins, then Dee put her arm around Grace and said, "Poor baby's led a sheltered life."

"I guess I have," Grace admitted.

Joey leaned over and whispered, "She's alerting you that the boss just walked in."

"And he is looking hunk-a-diddly-dumptious," Dee said, smacking her lips.

Grace laughed. "Oh, wait, three o'clock, I get it." She turned to her right and saw Logan, then quickly turned back and tried not to show she was flustered. "Does he come in every night?"

"He usually stops in, but never stays long," Dee said, then frowned. "Until recently, anyway. Last night he was here for a couple hours. Not sure what that's all about. I hope we're not getting laid off."

"The place is filled to capacity every week, so nobody's getting laid off," Joey said, then cast a less-than-subtle stare at Grace.

Dee frowned at him. "You think?"

"Oh, yeah," Joey said as he opened a new bottle of rum.

"What?" Grace said, glancing from one to the other.

Dee raised both eyebrows. "Has the boss got his eye on you, Gracie girl?"

She grimaced. "He just wants to catch me making a mistake so he can fire me."

"We'll make sure that doesn't happen, honey," Dee said, patting her shoulder. "Although, I gotta say, if I caught the eye of someone that hunkalicious, I'm not sure I'd be able to keep my cool." She waved a hand in front of her face. "Mmm-mmm. Is it getting hot in here or what?"

Grace elbowed her. "You're crazy."

"I don't think so," Dee said, chuckling.

"Here's your piña coladas, Gracie," Joey said. "You need help with the tray?"

"You're sweet, but I've got it."

"I'll say you've got it," Joey said, wiggling his eyebrows at her. "Now work it."

She laughed as she walked away with her drinks, fairly certain she'd never "worked it" in her life. But she was more than willing to try.

"I had three orgasms!" a woman cried.

Logan whipped around, shocked to recognize the young woman who'd been crying in the lobby yesterday afternoon. She had Grace wrapped in a fierce hug and she was jumping up and down.

Logan had just returned from an early-morning run up the peninsula and back. When he saw Grace walking toward the palmetto grove, he started to follow her, but her new best friend grabbed her first.

"Thank you, thank you," the woman gushed. "You were so right! He found that spot and it was miraculous!"

Fascinating. Logan watched Grace glancing around the

beach, probably checking to see if anyone had overheard the effusive woman. When she spied Logan standing ten feet away, she shook her head and closed her eyes in resignation.

Grinning, Logan continued to observe the exchange with interest, listening to every word as the woman gleefully described her husband's successful foray. It was clear now that Grace had instructed the young honeymooner on how to make love with her new husband. Very interesting.

His gaze narrowed and focused on her. It appeared that all those years Grace Farrell had spent studying the sexual and reproductive habits of spores and other creatures— including humans, obviously—had given her a level of sexual expertise he wanted to explore.

The thought made him grit his teeth. He wanted her right now. It was taking every ounce of control he had to not drag her into the palmetto grove, back her up against a tree and give in to the desire he knew they both felt for each other.

Grace hugged the woman and congratulated her, then watched her skip away. Once she was gone, Grace turned to Logan. "I suppose you heard all that."

"Pretty much."

"It's not what you think."

"Yeah?" he said. "Because I'm thinking you pretty much made her day. And night, apparently."

"Yes, well." She brushed her hair off her forehead, then fiddled with her sunglasses. "I didn't do anything she couldn't have… Well, I just…" She glanced up at the sky. "It's late. I really should get to my spores."

"Wait."

She froze and he took immediate advantage, stepping closer, invading her personal space.

"What is it, Logan? Is something wrong?" Her pink

tongue slid across her lush lips again and he almost groaned.

"If you lick your lips again," he warned, "I'm going to haul you over my shoulder and take you to my room."

She swallowed slowly. "I—I can't help it. You make me nervous."

"Do I?"

She glared at him. "You know you do. And I think you do it on purpose."

"Yeah, maybe I do." He skimmed his fingers across her shoulder and was gratified when she shivered. "That was a nice thing you did for her."

She tilted her head, clearly baffled. "You think so?"

"Yeah." His smile grew. "Do you often go around explaining the G-spot to clueless women?"

"Um, no." She shook her head slowly. "That was definitely a first."

He studied her, taking notice of the small scar over her left eyebrow, another smattering of pale freckles on the upper ridges of her cheeks, the perfect cupid's bow of her upper lip. "What the hell makes you tick, Grace Farrell?"

Puzzled, she said, "I might ask the same of you."

"Hey, I'm an open book."

A frown line marred her brow. "Not to me."

"The thing is," he said, "I'm usually a pretty easygoing guy. But ever since you showed up, I've been feeling a little edgy."

"That's not my fault," she said heatedly, poking her finger at his chest. "And I'm not leaving the island."

He grabbed her finger to stop the jabs. "It's not that kind of edgy." He kept hold of her hand, rubbing his palm against hers, shaping it and molding it to his.

"Oh."

"Yeah."

Awareness had her licking her lips again and a bolt of pure heat lit up his insides.

"What do you want?" she whispered.

"This." He leaned forward and kissed her, wrapping his hand around her nape to press her closer to him. Her mouth was as sweet as anything he'd ever tasted and he had to fight to keep the contact light. But his control was slipping as the heat of her body invaded his own. Visions of her lush, naked skin danced through his mind and he groaned.

He would've stopped, but a delicious sigh escaped her throat and her lips parted for him. He plunged inside her warmth and her tongue met his instantly, eagerly. Logan felt his heartbeat stagger and every muscle in his body hardened with need.

He wanted her, wanted to strip her clothes off and touch her breasts, her thighs, her slick core. He wanted his hands and mouth on every inch of her body. Now.

The images jarred him back to reality and he remembered they were standing outside in view of anyone who walked by. That's when he pulled back, but not completely. He took his time, kissing the corners of her mouth, her cheeks, the line of her jaw, the silky length of her neck.

"Let's go to my room," he murmured against her skin, then took her hand and started walking back to the hotel.

She stopped and pulled her hand away. "I can't do that. I have to go."

He turned and looked at her. "No you don't."

"I do. I'm sorry, I shouldn't have…" She paused to catch her breath. "You don't know me."

"No," he said carefully. "But I do know you want me and I want you."

She looked so serious. "You don't, really."

"You're wrong, Grace," he said, reaching for her.

She put both hands up to stop him. "If you really knew me, you never would've kissed me. You would've run for the hills." She took two steps backward. "I'm saving you the trouble."

"Nice of you."

"Oh, you have no idea." Then she gave a firm nod. "It's definitely best that we stop right now."

"Yeah?" He closed the gap between them. "I say we test that theory." Yanking her close, he covered her mouth with his and kissed her roughly at first. Then he softened his lips against hers and they moved together, deepening the kiss until they were both shaking with need.

When she moaned again, he let her go, then watched her lick her lips and taste him there. The move was innocent and skilled at the same time, and he scowled as an irrational wave of tenderness washed over him.

Finally, she opened her eyes and stared at him in wonder. "Wow."

"Yeah," he said gruffly. "That's what I'm talking about."

"Well, don't ever say I didn't warn you." Then she turned and jogged away as swiftly as her feet could move in the deep white sand.

He didn't follow her, just watched as she disappeared through the thick fronds at the far end of the beach.

What the hell was she talking about? He'd never had to work this hard to convince a woman to make love with him. *If you really knew me, you never would've kissed me.* He shook his head at the memory of her words. Oh, he knew her, all right. She was a woman and therefore a master manipulator. She could give lessons, no doubt about it.

That didn't seem to negate the fact that he was currently sporting a massive hard-on, thanks to her. Now that was something his entire staff would notice if he strolled into the hotel at that moment. So instead, he pulled off his shirt and tossed it on a chaise, then walked straight into the water to cool himself off.

Four

"Ladies and gentlemen," Logan said to the others participating in yet another conference call. "With the opening of the new Alleria sports center, the island will become a premier destination for world-class sporting events such as tennis, gymnastics and boxing."

Aidan, sitting in the brothers' penthouse offices two thousand miles away in New York City, picked up the conversation. "As you'll note in the prospectus we've sent you, the main court will have a tiered seating capacity of five thousand. We'll have ten deluxe private-viewing suites, a press booth, locker rooms, a four-thousand-square-foot commissary and private dining rooms for players and visiting dignitaries."

Eleanor, their senior vice president who was working out of the New York office with Aidan, jumped in. "There are six adjacent practice courts, as well. And the main court is easily converted to a boxing ring, gymnastic floor, a concert stage, or whatever is required. This project is shovel-ready, gentlemen. As soon as the contracts are signed, construction can begin."

"We've more than proven the viability of Alleria as a sports destination," Aidan said. "The Alleria Palms Golf Tournament is now third in worldwide television viewing audience, surpassed only by the Masters and the British Open. Our airport is world-class and we've recently expanded the resort by another five hundred rooms."

Part of the prospectus they'd sent their handpicked investors included a pictorial story of the island itself. It mainly featured their own bayside resort as well as the tiny Victorian port town of Tierra del Alleria. There, attractive shops and eclectic restaurants lined the beach and pier that formed the harbor where multimillion-dollar sailboats docked side by side with the local fishermen who sold their daily catch.

Logan and Aidan had created a ten-year, slow-growth plan to attract small businesses and specialty tourist groups. The sports center would attract the type of high-end traveler who, in theory, would appreciate the eco-friendly environment and rustic charm of the island.

There was silence on the line for a moment, then Tex McCoy spoke up. "You boys have got yourselves a pretty decent situation down there."

Logan had known Tex forever and could hear him puffing on his Cuban cigar as he participated in his favorite sport: wheeling and dealing. Logan could almost smell the thick, expensive cigar smoke. The billionaire Texan was one member of the consortium of wealthy investors who had invested in the brothers' past projects.

"You know you can count on me and my boys," Malcolm Barnett said amiably. "The wives are all itching to get back to Alleria since visiting this past year."

"That's always nice to hear, Malcolm," Logan said to the man who was regularly featured on the pages of *Forbes* and *Fortune*. Malcolm's two sons had gone to college with Logan and Aidan.

"Count me in, too," Tex said. "I'll have my people look over the contracts and get back to you."

Aidan said, "You know we appreciate it, Tex."

"Thank you, Tex," Logan chimed in. "You won't be sorry."

"You can both thank me by shaving a few points off my next golf game with y'all."

"Not sure we can do that, sir," Logan said with tongue in cheek.

"Sorry, Tex." Aidan chuckled. "We know you'd never want us to cheat."

The older man grumbled. "Damn your straitlaced father for raising such a pair of sticklers."

Everyone laughed, then several other investors jumped in to voice their desire to get in on the action. The conference call ended fifteen minutes later and Logan quickly called his brother on his cell phone.

"I think that went well," he said, grinning as he stated the obvious. Eleanor was probably in the New York office kitchen, popping open the champagne as they spoke.

Aidan ignored the statement. "What's going on with you?"

"What're you talking about?" Logan asked, stretching back in his chair. From here, he could see a catamaran drifting across the bay and wondered how soon he could get out of this suit and tie and into a pair of running shorts. "Everything's fantastic."

"I hear it in your voice, man. Something's bugging you."

"You're delusional," Logan drawled. "Everything's fine.

Perfect. We're about to close on a billion-dollar deal. Life is good."

Aidan paused, then said, "I'll drag it out of you eventually so you might as well save us both the trouble and tell me now."

Logan stared at the phone, wishing for once that he and his twin brother didn't have quite so tight a bond. It had been that way all their lives. They often finished each other's sentences and there were times when they could practically read each other's minds. They usually used it to their advantage, but right now, Logan didn't need anyone homing in on what he was thinking. Namely because he wasn't so sure of what was going on himself.

"Nothing's wrong, dude," he said, trying to convey a relaxed attitude he no longer felt.

Aidan snorted. "Fine, keep it to yourself, but I'll be back next Thursday and I expect to hear the whole story."

"Great," Logan said with a scowl. "I'll be sure to dream up something interesting to make you think you're right."

He disconnected the call and felt a twinge of irritation. He hadn't fooled Aidan one bit. But what was he supposed to tell him? How could he explain that a hot, sexy, spore-hunting research scientist had invaded their island and sucked up every last ounce of Logan's common sense?

He couldn't explain it. But once Aidan got here and saw Grace for himself, he would reach his own conclusions. Whatever his brother concluded, Logan intended to make it clear that Logan had seen her first and Grace Farrell was *his*.

Logan jerked forward and sat straight up.

"What the hell?" He shook his head in disgust. Where had that thought come from? He was rarely possessive when it came to women. In fact, he couldn't remember a time when he and his brother had been jealous of each other. It helped that they'd rarely ever gone after the same woman, but the few times they had, one of them had always acquiesced to the other. It just wasn't that important and, after all, there were plenty of women to go around.

But with Grace, Logan was willing to draw a line. It was mostly about business; after all, he and Grace had a deal. It was his responsibility to handle her situation. Aidan had nothing to do with it.

Okay, fine, he might be willing to admit that something about Grace tugged at him. The passionate way she'd defended her actions that first day still intrigued him. Logan sort of admired her quirky but logical way of thinking, even when it drove him nuts. And, he admitted, there was the basic fact that the woman was gorgeous.

"And scheming, and a liar," he added aloud, then shook his head in defeat. The schemes and lies didn't seem to matter. He still wanted to bury himself inside her.

Ever since that damn kiss he'd been unable to get her out of his mind. Several times he'd caught himself daydreaming, for God's sake, wondering what she was doing. Was she conducting a class in the joys of the G-spot to a new group of unsuspecting honeymooners? Was she hunting down spores in the rain forest? Was she balancing twenty-seven strawberry margaritas on her slim shoulders?

He thought about the other night in the bar, when Clive had trained her how to balance those heavy trays and she'd picked right up on his advice. Logan frowned with the sudden thought that Clive might be watching her a little too closely. He hoped not. He would hate to have to fire his top waiter.

He clawed his hands through his hair in frustration. Hell yeah, he was distracted, as Aidan had been quick to notice. But he was also discreet. Aidan would be the only person in the world who would have ever heard it in his voice. No one else would have a clue, and that's the way he wanted it. He didn't want or need anyone on his staff knowing his personal business. And, frankly, right now that included Aidan. Yeah, they were twins; but that didn't mean he was willing to kiss and tell, especially over the phone.

The main thing was, he didn't want Grace's reputation damaged. Not that he particularly *cared* about the woman one way or the other. He just *wanted* her. Once he'd had her, all these idiotic distractions would fade away and he would be able to get his head back on business and complete the sports-center deal.

In the meantime, Aidan would be home in three days and Logan was determined to have Grace Farrell for himself before that. It would help if he could just figure out a way to keep her from running in the opposite direction the next time he kissed her.

"Tequila, triple sec, sweet and sour, squeeze of lime," Dee said, and handed Grace a shot glass.

"Oh, I know this one," Grace said, taking a tiny sip. "Margarita, right? Mmm, that's good."

"That was too easy," Dee said, her tanned arm flexing as she lifted another bottle and poured. "I still can't believe you memorized the entire bartenders' guide but never tasted the drinks before."

Grace downed the rest of the margarita. "I suppose I've always been more of a reader than a doer."

"Guess those days are over," Dee murmured, grinning.

They faced each other at the small table in Dee's hotel room. Between them was a cocktail tray filled with different bottles that Joey had smuggled out of the bar for their enjoyment. But this was business as far as Grace was concerned. On the tray were chunks of fruit and several shot glasses, as well.

She had already taken sips of a martini, a gimlet, a Brandy Alexander, Sex on the Beach and a whiskey sour. She'd written the names down, followed by her own descriptions and reactions to the flavors of each drink, but her notes were looking a little fuzzy. Still, she was determined to learn as much as she could from Dee.

Mixing a new concoction in a clean shot glass, Dee slid it across the table. "This one's vermouth, bourbon and bitters."

Grace frowned as she tasted. "It's too strong."

"It's usually shaken with lots of ice and a cherry on top. Makes it really tasty."

"I hope so." She made a face. "Is that a Manhattan?"

"Yes," Dee said, sitting back in her chair and fluffing her long, dark hair. "You won't get a lot of orders for that down here since it's more of a big-city winter drink. But it's a classic."

"Then I should know how it tastes," Grace said firmly, and forced herself to take another sip. After almost a week of working together, she had finally confessed to Dee that she didn't have much experience as a cocktail waitress. Dee had wrapped an arm around Grace and revealed that everyone in the bar already knew that. Grace had begged for a few more tips about the job.

When Dee questioned her further, Grace had confessed that she rarely went out to bars and didn't really drink. That's when Dee had gleefully suggested they have a cocktail quiz.

"You might like this one better," Dee said, and handed her another tiny glass filled with a bright pink liquid. "Vodka, cranberry juice, lime juice and triple sec."

"Oh, I know this one," Grace said as she downed the

entire drink. "That's yummy, but I can't remember what it is."

"Cosmopolitan."

"Oh, yeah." Grace nodded slowly. "I get lots of orders for those. I can see why."

"They're smooth, but dangerous." Dee mixed another small cosmo and handed it to Grace, then put the caps back on all the bottles. "I think we're done."

"Oh." Grace frowned in thought as she stared at the notepad, trying to discern her scribbling.

"So you don't ever go out to bars, Gracie?"

"Not really," she said, and pushed her notepad aside.

"Do you have a boyfriend?"

"No." Grace grimaced. "I thought I did, but I was wrong."

Dee nodded sagely. "He was a jerk?"

"Oh, yes. Big-time."

"Goody," Dee said, rubbing her hands together. "Tell me all about him."

Grace laughed as she took a sip of her cosmo. "His name is Walter."

"Oh, sorry. But I have a creepy uncle Walter and that name is not a good sign," Dee said darkly. "He already sounds like a jerk, for sure. So how did you meet him?"

"You really want to know?"

"God, yes. Spill everything."

"Okay." She stretched her arms up for a few seconds, then pushed her hair back off her forehead, wondering where to begin. "Well, you know I work in a lab, and I've been so busy this past year that my boss decided to hire a new associate to help me. As soon as Walter started, we hit it off. It was nice, because we were spending long hours together. My experimentation phase was reaching a critical point." It was odd, but her tongue felt numb.

"Sounds very exciting," Dee said, sipping her mini-margarita.

"It was." Grace took a moment to remember how it was in the beginning. "Walter was wonderful. We talked about so many things. He seemed to really like me and he was always telling me how much he admired my intelligence."

"That's so sweet."

"It was," Grace said. "I don't get that a lot."

"Well, you should," Dee declared. She tried to rest her chin in her hand but her chin slipped twice before she was able to get comfy. "So keep going. I want to hear every last ghastly detail."

"Oh, it's ghastly all right," Grace admitted. "So, anyway, I suppose it was silly to be so flattered by Walter's attention, but he's very nice-looking and I've never had much of a love life before, so what did I know?"

"He took advantage of that."

"Yes. After two months of working together, he finally asked me out and I was over the moon. He took me out for a romantic candlelight dinner at a restaurant overlooking the lake. Then later when he took me home, he wanted to come inside. I was a little hesitant to let him in."

"It was your first date, right?"

"Right."

"He should've kissed you good-night and left."

"That's sort of what I thought. But he said we'd known each other long enough and he wanted to spend the night with me. Except he used a much cruder expression than that." She frowned, remembering that night. But at the moment, Walter's face in her memory was as fuzzy as her mind felt. She realized she liked him better that way. "Anyway, I told him I wasn't ready to take that step and he got angry. He said he knew I wanted it, so what kind of game was I playing? He said he'd spent almost two hundred dollars on me and wanted to get his money's worth. I ended up smacking him hard and while he was recovering, I ran inside my house and locked the door on him. He took it badly. Work became a nightmare with him around."

"Worse than a jerk," Dee said. "I hate him."

"Thank you. Me, too. But at the time, I felt like an idiot."

"It wasn't your fault," Dee said, jumping up and grabbing two bottles of water off the dresser. "He was a toad."

"I know." Grace popped open one bottle and took a long sip. "But I felt like such a cliché."

"Oh, been there, done that."

"Anyway, he finally quit, thank goodness, but he stayed in Minnesota. He's at a rival university and he's trying to claim my studies as his own."

Dee gasped. "What a total jackass."

"Yes, that describes him nicely." Grace couldn't sit still thinking about Walter, so she stood and walked over to Dee's window. She stumbled, but caught herself, then frowned at the rug, looking for whatever had tripped her. She didn't see anything. "I found out after he left that he'd stolen a small batch of my spores and some of my papers, and now he's applied for new funding to allow him to work on the exact same line of research as mine."

"Can we kill him?"

Grace blurted out a laugh. "Oh, Dee, you are the best."

"Hey, it's an option."

"I wish," she said, only half kidding. "No, all I can do is collect lots of new spores and continue my research when I get back. Thank goodness I never told him exactly where these rare spores could be found."

"A good thing for Walter," Dee said with a decided edge to her voice. "Because if he showed up here, he'd be very sorry."

"I really appreciate that," Grace said with a smile, then added, "even though you scare me a little."

She laughed. "I'll scare Walter a lot worse and that's a promise. I got your back, girlfriend."

Grace felt sudden tears prickling her eyes. Nobody had ever had her back before. Oh, she knew Phillippa would support her, if it came down to that. But somehow the way Dee had said it so simply and unconditionally, made Grace feel all warm and snuggly inside.

And even though she trusted Dee, she couldn't bear to confess the worst part to her. Yes, her university had promised to defend her against Walter's lies, but Grace knew that if she couldn't get the spores and raise the level of her research and experimentation to new heights, her reputation would suffer.

She also had to prove to the foundation that her work was her own and that she was the one deserving of the funds, not Walter. Otherwise, within a month she could lose her funding, her job and, most important, her reputation.

"Forget about stupid Walter," Dee said, interrupting her worries. "What about Mr. Hunkadelic?"

"What? Who?" Grace wondered if she'd had a few too many sips of Dee's cocktails because the lightning-quick change of subject made her head spin.

"You know who." Dee stared meaningfully at Grace. "The hunky man who is our boss? Mr. Big?"

"Oh, Logan." Grace stared intently at the label on her water bottle. The letters looked wobbly. Very odd. "What about him?"

"Something happening between you two?"

"Nothing."

"Then why aren't you looking at me?" Dee said, chuckling. "Do you have something to hide?"

Grace whipped around. "No! I mean…okay, he kissed me, but—"

"He kissed you?"

She sighed and flopped down on the bed. "Yes, and I warned him not to do it again."

"You…wait." Dee moved her chair so she could rest her feet on the bed. "Okay, I've got to hear your explanation for this one."

Grace stared at the ceiling as if help might be sent down from up above. But none came, so she finally met Dee's gaze. "It was for his own good."

"I don't get it. Is he a bad kisser?"

"Oh, no," Grace said, shaking her head. "He's really good."

"Well, then…"

"I ran away," Grace said, and buried her face in her hands. Humiliation swept through her. She still couldn't believe that she'd run from Logan like a teenager afraid of her own hormones.

Dee's eyebrows shot up and her feet thumped to the floor. "You ran away? Honey, are you crazy? Nobody runs away from Logan Sutherland. We're all running toward him."

She had known that, deep down of course. But hearing Dee say it out loud only confirmed that once again, Grace was "not normal." She didn't do anything like your average woman did. Heck, she hadn't even been able to stand her ground when a gorgeous man kissed her. It was pitiful. Just pitiful.

Still, she had to try to defend herself, pointless though it might be. "Dee, he doesn't know me. He's the one who would go running if he knew…"

"If he knew what?"

Grace gritted her teeth and forced herself to say it. "If he knew how smart I really am."

Dee came over to the bed, grabbed a pillow and sat next to her, resting her back against the headboard. "Honey, I confess I'm not sure how smart you are, but what does it matter? He kissed you. He likes you. Why are you running away from that?"

Grace folded her arms across her chest, anxious to make Dee understand. "Men don't like smart women."

"Oh, Gracie, that's just plain prehistoric. These days, men love smart women."

Grace shook her head stubbornly. "Not when they're as smart as I am."

Dee's mouth twisted in confusion. "Just how smart are you?"

"I have an IQ of 172," she said, annoyed with the slight whine in her voice.

"Oh, Gracie." Dee reached out and grabbed Grace's hand. "You realize that means nothing to me, right?"

"Yes," Grace said, laughing. "That's just one reason why I like you so much."

"I like you, too, Gracie," Dee said, "but really, is 172 good? I mean, what's average?"

"Well, that's difficult to say, really, since IQ scores have been gaining three points every decade now for some time, but—"

"Ballpark figure," Dee interrupted. "What's average?"

"About 100," Grace admitted with a sigh.

"Whoa." Dee blinked. "And what's genius?"

Grace groaned as she said, "One forty and above."

"Damn." Dee grinned at her. "So, you're like, what? *Über*genius?"

Stunned to discover that Dee's opinion of her hadn't

changed, Grace relaxed and for the first time in her life, actually giggled. "*Über*genius? I like that."

"You could be a superhero or something," Dee continued. "You could be Smartgirl!"

Relief and gratitude rushed through Grace as she returned Dee's smile. She had been so worried that once Dee knew the truth about Grace, she wouldn't want to be anywhere near her. After all, her own parents had run the other way from her, and that was a memory she really didn't want to dwell on just now. No, right now she wanted to concentrate on the amazing sensation of having her fears dissolve. For the first time, she was being accepted and liked, completely, for exactly *who* she was, not how *smart* she was—although Dee seemed to think that was pretty cool, too.

"Smartgirl? Sometimes I wonder," she muttered, then brightened. "But I do have four doctorate degrees."

"Wow! Four?" Dee laughed. "I lasted about six weeks in college. I was so bored, I ran screaming."

"Really?"

"Oh, yeah. So how long did it take you to get four degrees, cuz you look really young."

"I did all four of them concurrently."

"Wow." Dee shook her head, then took a sip of her drink. "Your classes must've been intense. But now you're like a PhD?"

"Yes, times four."

"Holy moley."

"I know," Grace whispered, then said, "Do you think we could have another mini-margarita?"

"I think I need one, too." Dee bounced off the bed and returned to the table to mix the drink. "So you work in your lab every day. But what do you do in your spare time?"

"I don't have much spare time," Grace said as she joined her at the table and squeezed a lime into the shot glass. "My work in the lab is very important, so—" she shrugged "—that's mostly what I do."

"Okay, I know you don't go out to bars," Dee said. "Do you like to shop or go to movies?"

"I've never really had much time to do either," Grace said, feeling more inadequate by the second.

"So you've only ever gone to school and worked in a lab?"

"That's pretty much it." She smiled cheerfully. "But I love my work."

"Oh, I like my job, too," Dee said, as she mixed another mini-margarita for herself. "But I like shopping, too, and, well, lots of things. But especially shopping."

"School and work are all I've ever known," Grace said, sipping her drink. "I started college when I was eight years old."

Dee's gaze was awash in sympathy. "That's terrible. College is hard enough on grown-ups, let alone a kid."

Grace blinked. She'd never shared that part of her background with anyone besides Phillippa. But that didn't mean there had ever been a moment when she'd considered herself unfortunate. Far from it. "I was lucky. I got to live at school and study and learn."

"Your parents let you live at school? When you were eight?"

"Well, I wasn't alone. I lived with the head of the Science Department and his wife."

"But your own parents sent you away?" Dee said.

"Oh, they were happy to do it," Grace said lightly. "I belonged in college. And it worked out well for them because the university paid them for me to go to school."

Dee stopped in midpour. "Your parents got money for you?"

"They didn't have a lot of money," Grace explained, "so I was glad to help them get by."

"But it sort of sounds like they sold you."

"Oh, no." Grace laughed. "I wanted to go."

"Gotta say, Gracie…I think somebody needs to go back in time and give your folks a swift kick or two."

"No, no," Grace said, pleased that her new friend would defend her, but knowing her parents had done the best they could. Maybe she hadn't quite understood it at the time, but now she knew that her mom and dad were nice, simple, hardworking people who had never understood her at all. "I appreciate it, but everything worked out."

"Wow," Dee said, taking an experimental sip, then another. "When I was eight, my big excitement was cutting all the hair off of my Barbie dolls. Guess we come from two different worlds."

"But we can still be friends," Grace said, hating to sound so tentative.

"Most indubitably," Dee said, giggling as she held her glass out in a toast. "We are friends, Gracie. Never doubt it. To my friend, Gracie."

"To my friend, Dee." Grace wiped away a happy tear as they clinked their glasses together.

Grace wasn't sleepy at all. So after leaving Dee dozing in her room, she walked out to the terrace and down to the beach. She couldn't get over how beautiful it was here, even at night. The moon was as big and clear in the sky as Grace had ever seen. The water was as smooth and shiny as the heavy-gauge stainless steel table in the lab's radiation room.

"You're hopeless," she muttered, shaking her head at

that comparison. Would her head always be stuck in the laboratory? She hoped not. She wanted to think carefree thoughts, dream frivolous dreams, like drinking champagne and kissing a handsome man under the Caribbean moon.

Had she always harbored a secret wish to be so frivolous? No, she was absolutely sure this was something new for her. But it felt good.

She hadn't drunk any champagne yet, but she'd had plenty of mini-margaritas. And as far as kissing a handsome man? Well, she'd done that, too, except for the moonlight part.

"And the part where you went scurrying away like a mouse," she reminded herself. Other than that, the kiss had been pretty darn dreamy.

The mild breeze whispered across her shoulders, ruffling her hair. Nudging her sandals off, she walked in bare feet through the cool sand. Oh, yes, she'd definitely had one too many mini-drinks, but she felt wonderful. At the water's edge she stopped, then had the strongest urge to keep on going. Touching the water with her toes, she discovered it was tepid. Not too cold, not too warm. Just right. And wouldn't it be delightful to swim in the moonlight?

"It's not safe to swim alone at night."

She whirled around. Logan stood behind her. "Oh, hello. I didn't hear you coming."

Logan came closer. "The sand swallows the sound of footsteps."

She smiled at his poetic words. "Are you taking a walk in the moonlight?"

"It appears I am."

"Isn't it beautiful?" she said, and spun around to take it all in.

Logan grabbed her before she stumbled straight into the shallow water.

"Oops," she said, and giggled.

"Have you had a few drinks tonight, Grace?" he asked as he pulled her closer to him. She wished he would smile again. He had such a nice smile. She couldn't seem to get it out of her mind.

Had he asked her a question? Oh, yes.

"I have," she said, resting her head on his chest because it seemed so inviting. "But it was strictly for business purposes. I was taking a test."

"A test?" he said, rubbing her back in a slow circle. "Which test was that?"

She could hear in the tone of his voice that he was smiling. She liked that tone, too, and gazed up at him. "Dee calls it the cocktail quiz."

"Ah. And how did you do?"

"I passed with flying colors because I'm very smart. Do you know how smart I am?"

"You've mentioned several times that you're very smart indeed," he said.

"But you don't know how smart I really am," she said, pointing her finger at his face, which was slightly blurry around the edges. "If you knew, you'd run for the hills."

"You said that before, too," he murmured, wrapping his hand around her finger. "But you're wrong."

"I think you're very handsome," she said, staring at him keenly.

He chuckled. "And I think you're toasted."

She thought about it, then nodded. "I think you're right. And I'm okay with that."

"Glad to hear it," he said, his arms wrapped securely around her waist. "Shall I walk you to your room now?"

She looked up at the night sky, then at him. "Aren't you going to kiss me again?"

"Do you want me to kiss you?"

"Yes, please," she whispered. "Under the moonlight, if you don't mind."

"Well, since you ask so politely…" He touched his lips to hers in a kiss so gentle, so sweet, so warm, Grace wanted to melt in his arms.

"Just like a dream," she uttered, feeling as if she were floating on air. Was she melting for real? She felt as light as a feather. Then she felt nothing at all.

Logan caught her as she slid downward, boneless and out cold. Lifting her effortlessly into his arms, he was thankful he'd decided to take a walk out to the beach to catch a few minutes of fresh air before heading to his suite for the night. Otherwise, he wouldn't have had a chance to rescue Grace from a night spent sleeping on the sand.

As he carried her across the terrace, he hoped like hell she wouldn't wake up with too bad a hangover in the morning. He had a feeling she didn't indulge very often, so she was probably going to pay for taking the cocktail quiz.

He reached her room and used his own master-key card to open it. Stepping inside, he let the door close behind him and carried her over to her bed to lay her down. Once she was settled, he glanced around her room and saw the elaborate setup she'd arranged on her table and across the top of her dresser. It was a portable laboratory complete with a serious-looking microscope, state-of-the-art laptop and some contraption with a toggle switch and digital read-out screen that measured something or other. There was a small scale next to a plastic thing that held glass cylinders suspended in a row, several of which had tubes attached that wound around and emptied into nearby beakers.

If he didn't know her better, he might've thought she'd set up a still to make whiskey.

He glanced back at Grace, who was snoring softly. She would probably freak out when she woke up in the morning and realized that her boss had been the one who'd carried her to bed.

She wore cropped pants and a thin blouse and he pondered the idea of taking her clothes off. She would sleep better wearing just her underwear, right?

He enjoyed the image of her waking up and seeing herself in panties and a bra. How quickly would she grasp that it had been Logan who'd undressed her?

Ah, well, it was a nice fantasy. One he wouldn't be carrying out tonight.

But soon. Very soon.

This time, though, he would allow her to keep her clothes on because that's the kind of guy he was. Pulling the lightweight comforter over her, he turned off the lights and left her alone to sleep off the cocktail quiz.

Five

He found her late the next morning, sitting in an over-stuffed rattan chair in the shady portion of the terrace. She wore dark glasses and a light pink sweater and was sipping something thick and red.

"Is that a Bloody Mary you're drinking?" he asked.

Grace looked up at him and tried to smile, but it was a bit shaky. "Dear God, no. No alcohol for me, thank you." She stared with suspicion at the concoction, then back at Logan. "It's something Joey mixed up. Supposed to be good for me because of my…um, hay fever."

"Hay fever." He grinned. "Is that what they're calling it these days?

"All right, fine," she said, pouting. "I'm a little under the weather. But it's all your fault."

He barked out a laugh. "My fault?"

"Of course."

"This I've got to hear." He sat in the chair next to her. "How is your hangover my fault?"

She turned slowly in her chair and faced him. "I was investigating ways to improve my job performance last night."

"Ah. And in order to improve your skills at carrying drinks, you got drunk, apparently deciding to carry those drinks on the *inside*. And since I'm the boss, it's my fault."

She frowned briefly. "Exactly."

He chuckled. "That's a new one."

She hunched a bit lower in her chair and glared at him. "It's true."

"Sweetheart, nobody said anything about you having to drink the same stuff your customers order."

"But I thought it would be good to know how the different drinks taste. That way I can give advice to people who ask for recommendations."

"That's thoughtful of you, but it doesn't excuse Dee from overserving you."

Grace grabbed his arm. "Don't you dare yell at Dee. She's my friend."

Logan's eyes focused on her soft hand on his arm. "I have no intention of yelling at her."

"Oh. Good." She pulled her hand back. "It's not her fault anyway. She didn't realize what a lightweight I am." She looked away. "Neither did I, I guess. And the drinks were in such tiny glasses, I never thought about how much I might be drinking and…"

The vulnerable look on her face almost did him in and he decided to change the subject. "Grace, do you remember seeing me on the beach last night?"

She frowned again, avoiding his gaze as she licked her lips. "I have a vague memory of that."

"Are you sure it isn't more than a vague memory?"

"Why?" she asked, turning to look at him. "Did I say something ridiculous? Should I apologize?"

"Of course not. You were on your best behavior. We had a nice conversation about the moonlight."

"Oh, good," she said with relief.

"And then you asked me to kiss you."

She cringed. "Oh, no." Then, taking a deep breath, she said, "Apparently I shouldn't be allowed anywhere near liquor without a keeper. I'm so sorry if I embarrassed you."

"You're kidding, right?" He regarded her intently. "The only thing I'm sorry about is that you were too tipsy to take the next step with me."

She flashed him a look he couldn't read because of those dark glasses blocking her eyes. But she seemed to dwell on his words, letting them sink in. He hoped so, anyway, because he intended to take that next step as soon as possible.

"What are you thinking, Grace?"

She cleared her throat. "Nothing much."

He scooted his chair closer to hers. "Are you thinking about that kiss? About what else we could share?"

She didn't answer, but he could see a faint blush rise on her pale cheeks.

"Because I'm thinking about it," he said softly, touching her shoulder with his fingers, then trailing a path up her neck and along her jawline. "I can't stop thinking about it. I want you in my bed, Grace, wrapped up in nothing but me. And once we're in bed together, I'll take my time with you. I want to touch and feel every inch of your body with my hands and my mouth and tongue. I want to make you feel everything I'm feeling. I want to make you hot. I want to make you scream."

Her breath shuddered out and she shifted uncomfortably in her chair. She swallowed hard and murmured, "Oh, God."

He leaned closer and whispered in her ear, "Say when,

Grace. Tonight? Say the word and we'll be together. To-morrow night? I won't wait much longer. I've got to have you soon." Then he bit her earlobe and soothed the bite with his tongue. "Yes?"

"Yes." She let out a soft moan. "Soon."

"Good." He touched her cheek, then stood. His body was tight and hard and he knew he'd suffer for an hour or more because of this little seduction scene. But it had been worth it. Even with the dark glasses covering her eyes, Logan could tell she had been as affected as he and that was, after all, the point. Right?

Smiling, he turned to leave. "You have a nice day, Grace."

She watched him walk away and had to resist the urge to call the hotel doctor. Her heart was stuttering so wildly from his incendiary words—not to mention that nibble on her ear—that she wasn't sure it would ever calm down again.

"Wow," she whispered. The man was potent. Maybe too potent. Because now she had to ask herself, was she ready for someone like Logan Sutherland? She had barely dated in the past ten years and after the debacle with Walter, she'd lost some confidence in herself as a woman. Of course, Logan's flattering words over the past few days had gone a long way toward helping her get some of that confidence back.

He'd also confused her completely. A few days ago, he'd made it more than clear that he didn't trust her. Lately, though, he seemed to have changed his mind. And today… She shivered again, then winced when her head pounded in response. Why had he chosen *today* of all days, to tell her he wanted her in his bed? She had been in no mental shape to argue him out of it. She certainly would have, she consoled herself, if she'd been able to.

But no, even she didn't believe that.

The memory of his mouth at her ear, his warm breath on her skin, made her feel nearly boneless with the want rampaging through her.

So now the question was, did she trust him enough to, well, allow him to do all those things his whispered promise had suggested?

Just thinking about giving herself up to him caused ripples of lust to waft through her stomach and roam even lower.

Oh, who was she kidding? She wanted him so much, she could barely sit still. She'd never felt this way about a man before, not even Walter. And she had trusted Walter!

"That proves you're a dunce," she muttered. She had trusted Walter and he had betrayed her, so how could she base her feelings for any man on the amount of trust she felt for him? She couldn't, so she might as well throw caution to the wind and do what she wanted to do. And, right now, all she wanted to do was Logan Sutherland. Heck, if she couldn't have trust, she would settle for lust.

"Yes," she murmured with a cautious smile. "Soon."

"He didn't mean it," she muttered to herself that night in the bar. She refused to be disappointed, chalking it up to her own naïveté when it came to men.

After garnishing four mai tais with pineapple chunks and maraschino cherries, Grace carried the cocktails over to one of her tables and passed them around to her customers.

She'd been on duty for four hours already and Logan hadn't shown up. After seeing his imposing presence in the bar every night for the past week, she was a little frustrated that he wouldn't show up tonight. Especially after propositioning her that afternoon.

If he didn't appear, should she go to his room? But what if he was with someone? Oh, God. She needed to forget he'd ever mentioned anything to her. Forget he'd whispered all those provocative suggestions in her ear. Forget the smoldering lust she'd been suffering all day.

He'd obviously been teasing her.

But why? Was he trying to set her up for a fall? If she came on to him, would he have his excuse to fire her? Was that his plan? If so, it was sneaky and mean.

It wasn't as if she wanted to work in the bar forever, but she had friends here now and she still cared about doing a good job. She had at least another week or two of spore collection before she would feel right about leaving, so she needed to protect herself against the possibility of losing her job.

So it was settled. She wouldn't act on her attraction to Logan. She'd already behaved like an idiot with one man. She didn't need to do it again. Walter had been handsome, too, although nowhere near as gorgeous as Logan. And look where her attraction to him had gotten her.

At least she and Walter had had something in common, for whatever that was worth. She and Logan, on the other hand, had nothing in common. He certainly had no interest in spores—that much was clear. Wasn't it important to have shared interests? What if he asked her about herself and she mentioned her fascination with biological dispersal and meiosis in the sporangium? His eyes would glaze over and he would zone out.

Of course, Grace was used to people outside of the lab dozing off when she began waxing microbiological. She could handle the general disinterest, although, privately, she didn't understand why the whole world wasn't utterly captivated by the subject of Allerian spores and their regenerative properties.

But she *really* didn't want Logan to do the zone-out thing with her. She wanted him to look at her and see more than a scientist. She wanted him to feel the same pulse-pounding desire that had been charging through her all day.

When she found herself staring out the window near the last table she'd served, she shook herself back to reality. She really needed to concentrate on her job or she'd find herself on the next plane off the island.

Back at the bar, she collected a larger order of ten drinks and arranged them on a tray. After a few deep breaths to keep her nerves at bay, she whispered the words that always helped relax her. "Helium, argon, xenon."

Positioning her feet on the floor and flexing her leg muscles as Clive had taught her, she lifted the tray in one smooth movement onto her shoulders. Then she blinked. "Wait, neon comes before argon. And Krypton comes before... Oh, dear."

She steadied the tray and began to walk carefully toward her next table. She would have to take extra care with her drink trays tonight because she was obviously flustered. Otherwise, she never would've mixed up the order of noble gases in the periodic table. She forced herself to concentrate as she crossed the room, talking to herself as she walked. "Now where was I? Oh, yes, krypton, xenon, radon. Now the alkali metals. Lithium, sodium, potassium—"

"Looking good, Gracie girl," Dee said with a wink as she passed her in the aisle between tables.

"You, too, Dee." Grace grinned. She'd never had a friend like Dee before, someone who was smart and funny and so much fun to talk to. Grace's closest friend in Minnesota was Phillippa, and while they had a good time at work together, Grace didn't have many friends outside of the lab. Not a friend like Dee, anyway. She hadn't known her long but already felt so close to her.

Grace didn't know what she'd do without Dee, once she went back to Minnesota. They could email, of course, but that wasn't the same. The thought depressed her enough that she had to put it out of her mind. For now, she would think positively. She was here on the island because of the spores, of course, but Dee was near the top of her list of best reasons to come back to Alleria someday soon.

Grace made it to her customers' table and back to the bar before she realized she'd forgotten to name the rest of the alkalis.

What was wrong with her? It was a good thing she'd gone back to her room to rest for a few hours that afternoon. Lord knows how much more loopy she'd be tonight without that nap. She vowed never to overindulge again, knowing what a mess it made of her memorization skills, among other things.

A low-level buzz stirred its way through her system and Grace turned around to see what was causing it.

Logan.

Glancing around, she realized nobody else in the room was taking an interest in his presence but her. Where in the world had that buzz come from? She didn't know, but her insides were tingling and the pale hairs on her arms were standing up.

He stood a few feet inside the doorway and stared at her with an intensity that nearly had her knees collapsing. As she gripped the edge of the bar, he jerked his chin toward the door. Did that mean he was leaving?

"I'll take over your tables," Dee whispered in Grace's ear as she took hold of her drink tray. "Go."

Her friend nudged her away from the bar and Grace stumbled toward the door where Logan stood waiting. The bar crowd became a vague shadow and the raucous laughter faded to a soft drone. All she saw was him.

Heart pounding, she met him at the door. Were his eyes always that compelling, she wondered. Or was tonight special? Was there something more in the way he looked at her? She saw the tension in his features and knew he was experiencing everything she was. The sexual pull between them was off the charts, no matter what periodic table she might use to try to define it.

But oddly, Grace had zero interest in quantifying anything that lay between them. The fact that their feelings for each other existed was enough. The look in Logan's eyes said it all. He'd come for her. He'd meant what he said. He wasn't setting her up for a fall or trying to fire her. He wanted her. And in that moment, all her earlier worries dissolved. She knew she was safe with him.

He took her hand and they strode out of the bar side by side. She gazed up at him and thought, *well, not exactly safe*. She was in over her head. She knew it. She'd never been with a man like Logan Sutherland before and barely knew her next move. But she *was* a genius, after all, so she would surely figure it all out soon.

And if not, she would never let him know it.

Her scent enveloped him and fueled his craving for her. Logan had almost stayed away tonight, thinking she'd come up with some excuse to refuse him. But in the end, he had to see her. It didn't mean anything. *Couldn't* mean anything. It just meant that he needed a woman and she was the one his body happened to require.

It barely registered that some of his staff were watching him. He'd noticed Dee taking Grace's tray, knew they were friends and he was grateful for it. As for the others, if his behavior stirred up any gossip among them, they would have to get over it.

As Grace walked toward him, he was pitifully glad he'd come. Her thin sarong was backlit by the lights of the bar and Logan could see the outline of her gorgeous legs as she sauntered toward him. His gaze was riveted to the apex of that silhouette, the subtle brush of those slender thighs as she moved closer, the curvaceous shape of her hips, the subtle rise and fall of her breasts that seemed to signal her own need.

She'd worn her dark red hair loose tonight and it fell in bouncing waves over her shoulders. He wanted to gather it in his hands and bury his face in those lustrous locks while he lost himself in her hot core.

It took every bit of control he had—control that slipped with every step they took together—not to lead her into the nearby utility room, pull off her bikini bottom, thrust himself inside her and quench this hunger. But the cold wall of a janitor's closet wouldn't do for their first time together. He intended to spend a long, long time savoring her—and for that, he wanted complete privacy. And a damn strong mattress.

They entered his suite and he wasted no time. As the door clicked closed, he flipped the lock, then turned and lifted her into his arms, giving in to the need to hold her again as he had the night before. With her pressed against him, he could recall all over again the feminine softness of her body skimming his hard chest.

She wrapped her arms around his neck and nestled her head against his shoulder as he moved quickly through the front salon and into the bedroom. Once there, he covered her mouth in a hot, devouring kiss that she met with equal fervor. Then he placed her gently on the bed and watched as her eyes searched his face and her arms reached out for him.

"Come to me," she said. It was the first time she'd spoken since he'd grabbed her hand and led her out of the bar. Now, as he stared hungrily at her lips glistening wet from their kiss, he knew he was about to reach the end of his famous control.

Kneeling on the bed, he straddled her, took hold of both her hands and pulled her arms up over her head. The action caused her breasts to thrust out for his pleasure. He reached behind her back to untie her bikini top, then slipped it over her head and tossed it aside. He stopped and took a moment to gaze at her exposed, perfect breasts.

"Gorgeous," he muttered, taking both breasts into his hands to mold them gently, using his thumbs to stroke her rosy nipples to stiffness.

He bent to take one nipple into his mouth, sucking gently, licking and teasing it with his teeth and tongue. Then he switched his attention to her other breast, plying her sensitive nipple with sensual nips and licks until she moaned deep within her throat. She was writhing beneath him now and he slid himself up to claim her mouth in another kiss so heated, it could end things here and now if Logan didn't force himself to step back and slow down.

He untied the knot of her sarong and pushed it aside, then slid his fingers under the edge of her bikini bottom, seeking her most intimate spot. When he slid one finger inside her, she groaned in need.

"Tight," he murmured. "And so hot." He eased another finger in, then moved both fingers out and back in again as her flesh grew even more heated and moist with her need.

"Logan," she whispered. "Please."

Her hair moved in waves around her head like a dark red halo and her intoxicating taste and scent filled his senses. As her sweet body twisted against him, tempting him beyond the edge, his mouth sought hers blindly, renewing his claim on her. His hard length pressed against her, demanding entry.

"I need to have you now," he said, barely recognizing the uncivilized rumble in his voice.

"Yes, yes," she urged him.

He jumped off the bed and quickly removed his clothes. Reaching into the top drawer of his dresser, he grabbed a condom and slipped it on.

Then he returned to her, yanked her bikini bottom down and threw it across the bed. Grasping thick strands of her hair in his hands, he urged her to meet his gaze. "I want you too much, Grace. It'll have to be hard and fast this first time."

She nodded, her eyes glazing with desire. "Yes."

"Finesse will have to come later."

"God, yes, just touch me," she demanded, lifting her mouth to cover his in a kiss so laced with sweet passion it brought an unfamiliar ache to his chest; and it forced him to ease back on his relentless urge to lose himself inside her.

Instead, he kissed her again, meeting her sweetness with his own demanding assault on her mouth, her lips, her tongue. Finally, though, that kiss, as deep as it was, wasn't enough to stay him any longer. He broke free, pulled his head back and stared down at her.

"Look at me," he whispered. "I want to see you lose control with me."

She complied and he stared with masculine satisfaction at the fierce glimmer of heat and need in her eyes. Holding her gaze, he plunged into her with one strong thrust.

She gasped and her eyes widened in shock.

"What the hell?" he shouted, then grimaced as he fought to hold himself completely still.

"Don't stop," she insisted, wrapping her arms around his waist. She lifted both legs, resting her thighs against his hips, and that movement beneath him was a sensual wave that threatened to consume his last ounce of brainpower.

But Logan forced himself to stop anyway, his eyes locked on hers as he struggled to speak. "You're a virgin?"

"That's not really important right now," she said tightly, and raised her hips to urge him deeper inside her.

"But…the G-spot," he uttered, resting his forehead on hers as he focused every ounce of his energy on keeping perfectly still. "What about when you—"

"Can we discuss this later?" she said, and wound her legs around his to keep him bound to her.

"You're killing me," he said with a groan.

"Don't make me," she said through clenched teeth.

"When did you get so pushy?" he said, biting back a grin as he reached out and smoothed a strand of hair away from her cheek.

She sighed. "Nobody warned me that men talked so much during sex."

He laughed despite the awkwardness of the moment. "Fine, but we're going to have a long talk afterward."

"I figured we would."

He began to move again, slowly at first, then with building speed. He tried to keep his strokes long and smooth in order to ease inside her without causing too much pain. But when she skimmed her hands across his back and locked her legs around his waist, he lost whatever last bit of control he'd managed to maintain thus far.

She matched him move for move and her heart pounded in rhythm with his. He pushed harder, pumped faster as they both climbed higher, his need igniting more and more with every thrust.

She rocked against him and Logan drove into her with savage delight, stroking and gliding as she urged him on. Then, with a sudden sharp intake of breath, she uttered his name and shattered beneath him.

Logan watched her surrender in his arms and an innate need to join her overtook him. Thrusting harder, faster, deeper, his breath grew ragged as he used every muscle in his body to push again, then again, until an explosive wave of pleasure engulfed him and he was hurled over the edge with Grace.

Exactly where he most wanted to be.

Six

Grace wasn't sure how long she slept. Eventually, she opened her eyes and found Logan leaning on his elbow, watching her. A frown marred his handsome features.

"I hurt you," he said, as his fingers edged along her hairline. He was still stretched out next to her with his leg thrown over hers. It felt perfect.

"No," she said, struggling to sit up and regain some dignity. But it was impossible because he wouldn't budge, so she plopped her head back down on the pillow with a sigh. Dignity was overrated anyway. Besides, she was *naked*. How much dignity would she really be able to find?

And who really cared? She had finally lost the big V she had carried around inside her mind for years. Her virginity was gone and frankly, she had never expected to enjoy losing something so much. Grace looked up into Logan's eyes and felt her heart give a soft, warm flutter. He had been wonderful, even though, right now, he didn't exactly look pleased to be her deflowerer.

"You didn't hurt me at all, Logan. It was…"

"Why didn't you tell me?" he asked.

It would be silly to pretend not to know what he was referring to, but she considered playing dumb for a half second. Then she gave it up. "You mean why didn't I tell you I was a virgin? Honestly, I didn't think it would be an issue. And I confess I was so wrapped up in the moment, I didn't want to stop. I'm glad we didn't stop."

He smiled at that. "Me, too, Grace. But I still wish you'd said something." His voice was repentant as he stroked her hair. "I would've been more gentle, taken my time to make you feel more at ease."

She was surprised to see regret reflected in his eyes and she reached up and touched his face. "You did everything right, Logan. It was wonderful."

"No," he said meaningfully, taking hold of her hand. "But it will be."

He lowered his mouth to hers, kissing her with a tenderness she'd never thought to experience. Desire trembled within her all over again, rising inexorably as he tormented her with gentle warmth, lavished her with whispered endearments, tempted her with slow, openmouthed kisses. He touched her with a softness born from regret, she knew, that he'd neglected to use enough care with her before.

The sweetness of his actions touched her heart and she met his passion with a wholehearted joy she'd never known before. Oh, she tried to hold on to a dash of detachment for her own good, but it was useless. Logan effectively destroyed all her defenses until she was left with nothing but shivering need for his hands and mouth on her skin.

Was this what love felt like? Oh, she wasn't stupid enough to imagine she'd fallen in love with him. But she'd often heard that being in love was the best feeling in the world, and right now, she felt pretty darn fabulous.

"I'm just going to hold you for a while, Grace," he said softly, tucking her in close to his side.

"We're not going to—" Even she could hear the disappointment in her voice.

He smiled against her hair. "Not right this minute."

"Oh," she said, snuggling her head against his shoulder. "Why?"

Logan chuckled and she smiled even as she closed her eyes.

"Because you wore me out, Grace," he said, still smiling.

"I did?" She sighed, and stretched out one arm across his broad chest. Even though it had been her first time, she must have done everything right. Good to know. "That's nice."

As they dozed off to sleep, she issued her naive self a warning. This wasn't love. She hoped she was smart enough to know that much. But several times during the night, when she awoke and found herself in his arms, she had to wonder if she hadn't already slid effortlessly into something very close to love with him.

As daylight began to lighten the room, Grace quietly rose from the bed and got her first real look at Logan's elegant bedroom. Pale gold walls and terra-cotta floor tiles gave the space a lovely, open feeling, while thick, colorful area rugs provided warmth and a touch of charm. White plantation shutters covered a wall of windows that when opened would no doubt reveal an unsurpassed view of blue water and lush green hillsides. A comfortably overstuffed taupe sofa with striped brown and coral pillows sat against the wall facing the bed. The room was casual, elegant and expensive, and completely suited its owner.

Logan sprawled sound asleep under the covers, all rumpled and warm and sexy. Shards of sunlight streamed in through the windows illuminating the king-size bed and lending a romantic aura to the scene.

"No, no," Grace whispered, taking quick pains to sweep all thoughts related to romantic auras out of her mind. What she and Logan were having was sex. Wild, exciting and passionate, for sure, but not a romance. Romance was for some other couple, not for them. And that was just fine and dandy with Grace. She could be as sophisticated as the next girl, right? So she vowed to be perfectly happy and enjoy her time with Logan for as long as it lasted.

And once she was back in Minnesota, whenever she found herself feeling a little bit lonely, she would be able to look back at these moments with him and remember this time as the most thrilling of her life.

Not everyone could say they'd had such a time. She was lucky. And happy.

She took one more glance at Logan, then tiptoed to the bathroom. Staring at herself in the mirror, she gave herself a little squeeze because she felt so wonderful. She'd never guessed that sex could be so... Well, now she totally understood why the spores did it every morning like clockwork.

She finished freshening up, then quietly opened the bathroom door. And shrieked.

"Not staying for coffee?" Logan said casually, as he stood there waiting for her. He wore a gorgeous smile, but otherwise, he was completely naked.

She scurried backward and yanked a bath towel off the rack to wrap around herself. Naked in the middle of the night while she was wrapped around him was one thing. Naked while standing in the morning sunlight having a conversation was something else altogether. "I didn't think you'd… Well, good morning."

"Good morning to you," he said, still grinning. "You do know I saw your naked body all night long, Grace."

"That was different," she said, clutching the towel in a death grip. "Now it's…it's morning." She almost groaned. So smart, yet, oh, so lame.

"Yes, it is," he said agreeably. "I ordered coffee and breakfast. No need to rush off."

"Oh, thank you. But I should…" She had no idea how to complete that sentence. Her lack of knowledge when it came to sexual etiquette was disheartening.

"Stay," he said, settling the matter. He walked past her into the bathroom. "I'll be right out."

They had breakfast on his private terrace. He'd ordered eggs, bacon, sausage, hash browns and toast for both of them, along with a variety of pastries, juice and coffee.

Grace knew she wouldn't be able to eat half of the food on her plate, but took a bite of egg and a sip of coffee.

One half hour later, her plate was empty and Logan was pouring her another cup of coffee.

"I guess I was hungry," she said, as she stirred a teaspoon of cream into her coffee. Logan had graciously loaned her his bathrobe so she would feel more comfortable.

He stretched back in his chair. "It's refreshing to be with a woman who enjoys eating as much as you do."

"I take it you haven't been up to Minnesota lately," Grace said wryly. She popped the last bite of toast into her mouth and dabbed her lips with her napkin.

He laughed. "You're right…I haven't."

"We have to eat to stay alive up there," she explained. "And we live by those words. Minnesotans believe you need an extra layer of body fat or two, just to keep warm through the long winters."

"Ah." He leaned closer, untied her bathrobe and skimmed his fingers across her stomach, causing a shiver of excitement to race through her like lightning. "But you don't have an extra layer of body fat on you, Grace."

"I...I suppose I work it off in the lab." She wished she could drag him back to bed right then. But, once again, she had no idea what constituted proper behavior the morning after.

"Your lab job sounds like it would be fairly sedentary. Is it?"

"I suppose it can be for some people, but I do a lot of running around."

They both reached for the same croissant and she almost screamed from the shock of tingling heat she felt as their hands touched. What was wrong with her?

She stared at Logan but he didn't seem to be at all affected by the touch. Instead, he grinned, took the croissant, tore it and handed her half.

"So tell me why someone like you is still a virgin."

The question surprised her. "Someone like me?"

He broke off a piece of the flaky pastry and munched on it. "You're beautiful, Grace. What's wrong with the guys up there in the tundra? Has all that snow frozen their brains?"

"Maybe." She felt her cheeks warm up, but she had to smile at the unexpected compliment. "Thank you. But the most likely answer is that the men I work with are lab geeks like me. They're only interested in my theories."

She wasn't about to tell him how Walter had pretended an interest he didn't really feel. Instead, she added, "Other than that, I don't get out of the laboratory much."

"Why not?"

"It's my job," she said simply, but it was more than that. "It's my life."

"Life is more than a job," he countered.

"I suppose it should be," she said, and knew she could've left it at that. But, for some reason, she wanted him to know more about her. "But I grew up there. I'm most comfortable when I'm surrounded by science. Even though much of it is theoretical, it's so much more real than anything else in my life. It's tangible. I totally understand it, too. It's nothing like the world outside the lab where everything is confusing and I always feel like I don't know the rules." And that sounded pathetic, didn't it? She took a breath and added, "The lab is safe—and unemotional, for the most part. Except when I get excited about some result or finding."

He studied her as he sipped his coffee. "What do you mean, you grew up there?"

She shrugged. "I've lived at the university since I was eight."

"Eight?" His eyes narrowed and he set his coffee cup down and leaned in. "You mean, eight years old?"

On the other hand, maybe she shouldn't have been quite so forthcoming because now he was staring at her as if she'd suddenly grown a second head. Her imagination took flight as she envisioned the headlines: *Two-headed scientist found on tropical island.* Eyewitness reports would deem it scientifically significant, but gruesome nonetheless. She and her two heads would be put in a cage and displayed at zoos around the world. And everyone would look at her the way Logan was right this minute.

Grace reeled her thoughts back to planet Earth and held her chin up high. "That's right, I was eight years old. I told you I was smart."

"Yeah, you did," he said slowly, sitting back and crossing one leg over the other. "Told me I'd run for the hills if I knew how smart you really were."

"That's right. Well…" She folded her napkin, placed it carefully on the table and stood. "I'll be going now."

He grabbed her hand. "Not so fast, Grace."

"Logan, I think we've said all there is to say."

"I don't." He yanked her down onto his lap and met her mouth with his in a hard, wet kiss that involved teeth and tongues and lots of zapping electrical currents zooming through her body. Then he pulled his mouth away and she knew she would've collapsed if he hadn't been holding her so tightly.

"I may not be Einstein," he said gruffly, his eyes narrowed on her, "but I'm not an idiot. I like you just fine. And I don't run."

Looking into his eyes, all she could think was that she was the one who probably should run—but she really didn't want to. As soon as she caught her breath, she whispered, "I'm glad."

"Good." Then he grinned. "Now let's go hunt for spores."

She had been a virgin.

Logan was still shaking his head in disbelief two days later as he sat at his office desk. He'd just received the revised set of blueprint renderings of the proposed sports center and he pulled them from the large mailing tube. Unrolling the thick stack of drawings across his conference table, he used his stapler and a hardbound dictionary to secure the ends and prevent the stack from curling up.

Grace was the last woman on earth he would've guessed would be a virgin. If he'd known, he sure as hell wouldn't have taken her to bed the other night.

But how could he have guessed? The woman had come

across as though she'd written the book on sex. She studied a species' sexual habits, for God's sake. She gave lectures to newlyweds on how to find their G-spot—or whatever they were calling it these days. Who would've guessed that Ms. Sexual Expert had been faking it this whole time?

"Hell." He wiped a hand across his jaw. He should've been pissed off with her deception, but instead he caught himself laughing out loud as he recalled her demands in bed the other night. He'd tried to be a nice guy when he discovered she'd never done the deed before. He'd been willing to stop altogether, or at least slow down. But not Grace. She was full steam ahead. Thank God.

Logan shook away the image of Grace naked in his bed and tried hard to focus on the sports center blueprints.

He and Aidan had learned long ago that projects like the sports center would cause problems at every step. And whenever a new problem reared its ugly head, a whole new set of drawings had to be rendered. So not only had the design of the center itself changed three times now, but they'd been forced twice to completely move the site of the project. The new site was based on the latest geological survey and the environmental impact reports they'd received last month.

Logan turned to the next blueprint to study the architect's three-dimensional rendering.

Most of the problems with building a sports center on the tiny island of Alleria had to do with the geological makeup of the island itself. The beaches, the natural bay and the rocky coves were the features that brought most of the tourists here. But also, the island had been formed by an ancient volcano, now dormant, and the land around the volcano had been ravaged by ancient lava flows. Now, over one square mile of north island coastline was barren except for the scrub that managed to grow there. In contrast, much of the southern part of the island was covered in lush rain forest.

The original investors had suggested that the brothers put the sports center adjacent to the hotel and within walking distance of the edge of the rain forest. The theory was that sports enthusiasts would be able to enjoy not only the beauty of the rain forest, but also the hiking and zip-line features offered.

But early on, Logan and Aidan had nixed that location and considered canceling the entire project. Who wanted to look at or spend time at a concrete sports center when they could simply enjoy the natural beauty of the island itself? But when the brothers decided they could relocate the sports center to the north side of the island, closer to the dead zone at the foot of a dormant volcano, the project was revived and revamped.

The brothers wanted a hotel built closer to the sports center, as well. They had invited developers to the island to check out the possibilities, but none of those builders had brought the sort of entrepreneurial spirit and sensibility that Logan and Aidan envisioned for their island. But then, this past year, they'd met their Duke cousins for the first time.

Adam, Brandon and Cameron Duke owned Duke Development and after touring a few of their California properties, the Sutherland brothers had decided that the Dukes would be the perfect partners in a new boutique hotel on Alleria.

The Duke family would be arriving next weekend and Logan and Aidan had already planned an extensive private tour for them in order to show off all the special qualities that had originally attracted them to Alleria.

In fact, there were several island features that had never been advertised in the hotel brochures or on the website, such as the hot springs that bubbled in various places around the island. The ancient volcano had created thermal pockets that still provided heat to the small pools. One secluded lagoon was located in the rain forest, within hiking distance of the hotel. But the hike was treacherous enough that few hotel guests had ever ventured far enough into the forest to discover it.

Logan suddenly wondered if the scientist in Grace would enjoy exploring the hot springs. Logan grinned, knowing the scientist in *him* would definitely enjoy exploring her naked body as it soaked up the heat.

"Damn," he muttered. It was getting impossible to concentrate on work as the thought of Grace crossed his mind again. She was definitely unlike any virgin he'd ever known before—not that he'd known all that many. Frankly, he tried to avoid virgins whenever possible. They were just too much damn responsibility. After all, if he somehow ruined a woman's first sexual experience, it would traumatize her for the rest of her life and leave a black cloud over her memory of him and all other men on the planet. Who needed that kind of pressure? Not Logan.

Grace didn't seem at all traumatized, he thought, then chuckled. Far from it. In fact, Logan had been blown away by her natural passion and enthusiasm for trying new things. He had originally planned to walk her back to her hotel room later that night; but, the truth was, he hadn't wanted to let her go. The feel of her in his arms, the soft sigh of her breath as she drifted into sleep. The woman got to him on levels he hadn't even been aware of.

They'd spent every night since then together.

He couldn't get enough of her and damned if he knew what to make of that.

The only thing that concerned Logan was that once his brother and their corporate staff returned to Alleria, he was a little uncertain about how he and Grace would arrange to spend time together. Getting their latest project up and running was going to keep both Logan and Aidan busy.

But, hell, maybe it wouldn't be an issue; his need for Grace might fade by then. It would certainly fade eventually. It always did. And, of course, sooner or later, she would have to go home. And that would be the end of it.

But that didn't matter right now. For now, he wanted her in his bed at night. Once Aidan was back, Logan and Grace would simply have to be as discreet as possible. After all, he didn't need his brother tormenting him about sleeping with the staff. On the other hand, Grace wasn't really part of the staff anyway, considering the fact that she'd arrived on the island under false pretenses. So it wasn't a problem, was it?

Yeah, that was his story and he was sticking to it.

"I still can't believe you've never been sailing before," Logan said as he held Grace's hand and helped her aboard the sailboat.

"The closest I ever got was when I very young and went fishing with my father."

Logan watched her glance around and take everything in. "How'd that go for you?"

She stepped up next to the mast and studied the rigging and hardware. She seemed to be weighing her words before she finally gazed at him and spoke. "I spent most of the time calculating the velocity of the wind versus the barometric pressure, then trying to angle my fishing line in the direction I'd theorized would produce more biting fish."

Logan laughed as he hauled the large picnic basket on board, then led the way down into the cabin. The thirty-foot Catalina sailboat belonged to Logan and Aidan and they'd had some great adventures—and some awesome parties—sailing around the Caribbean together. But with business obligations and scheduling problems, it had been a few months since Logan had taken the boat out.

Grace followed him down and glanced around the sleek main cabin. "It's so nice down here."

"Yeah, it's a cool design," he said, strapping the picnic basket under the galley table.

"So did you catch any fish?" he asked.

"Yes, I caught twelve," Grace admitted, frowning.

"Twelve fish for a little kid is a pretty good haul," he said, flashing her a grin. "How'd your dad do?"

She made a face. "He didn't have much luck. He told me I scared the fish away."

Logan was taken aback. "Hardly sounds fair."

"It wasn't his fault," she said quickly. "I talked a lot. I guess it freaked him out sometimes."

"What do you mean?" He climbed the ladder back up to the deck, then turned and gave her a hand up.

"I was such a pain," she said with a rueful laugh. "I seemed to know so much about everything, except I didn't know enough to shut up once in a while. Little kids like to talk, you know? But my parents didn't seem to have a clue what I was talking about. I intimidated both of them."

She said it lightly, but Logan could see the hurt in her eyes. He could relate to the pain she must still be suffering from her parents' inability to love and understand their child.

"I thought parents love it when their kids are smart." He tossed her a life jacket and she slipped it on over her tank top. "Their reaction doesn't sound right."

She sighed. "When I was five years old, my cat broke her leg and I set it in a plaster cast. My parents took the cat to the vet to have it x-rayed and he said it was a picture-perfect set."

Logan laughed. "Wow, they must've been proud of you."

"Oh, no, that scared them to death."

"I can't believe that. I mean, there are plenty worse things you could've done. At least you used your power for good."

"I tried," Grace said, laughing, then sobered. "My parents used to say that I belonged to the world. I think it was their excuse to get me out of the house because they didn't know how to deal with me."

"You don't seem all that difficult to deal with."

She smiled and stared out at the water, but Logan had a feeling her thoughts were a few thousand miles away. After a moment, she turned and looked at him. "I've never admitted this to anyone, but when they told me I was going to go live at the university, I was scared to death. I cried and begged them not to send me away. I promised I'd behave better, but they insisted that it wasn't about my behavior. It was about me having this great opportunity. That was how they justified it, I guess, by telling themselves they were doing it for me. But they looked so relieved and happy about their decision, I knew they'd simply given up on me. So I let them think I was excited to be going."

"Sounds like you were the grown-up in that house."

"Maybe."

"I'm so sorry."

She shook her head and waved his words away. "No, I'm sorry. Nobody likes a whiner."

"Grace." He sat down, took her hand in his and said quietly, "Don't apologize. Tell me what it was like for you at school."

She smiled. "You don't want to hear all that melo-drama."

"Tell me."

"Okay," she said, and took a deep breath. "At first it was awful. I was afraid every day, and I was so lonely. I had no friends my own age and everyone looked at me like I was an alien or something."

"Did you tell your parents?"

"Oh, no," she said quickly. "I knew they didn't want to hear anything bad. But it turned out okay. I loved work-ing in the laboratory, and, slowly but surely, the university became my life. It's where I belong."

She gazed up at him and tried to smile. "I guess I sound pretty weird, don't I?"

Logan shrugged. "Who isn't weird?"

She beamed at him and squeezed his hand. "That's so nice of you to say."

"Hey, it's true. And trust me, I'm not that nice." He stood and stepped onto the pier to untie the rope, then shoved the boat off and jumped back onto the deck. "Just watch me turn into Captain Bligh."

Saluting, she said, "Aye aye, Captain."

Logan used engine power to steer the boat through the small marina and out into the bay, explaining the basics of sailing to Grace and assigning her certain duties. As soon as they cleared the last pier, he unfurled the sails and they headed for open water.

It had taken every ounce of willpower he had to stay calm as Grace talked about her parents. He couldn't imag-ine growing up in a house like that. Hell, his own mother had walked out when he was seven, but at least he and his brother had always had their father. Dad had been their biggest champion and always showed them nothing but love and support, even when they behaved badly.

But Grace's parents? Sounded like all they'd shown her was contempt. They'd never supported her at all. In fact, it sounded like they might've tried to stifle her constant search for knowledge; but, knowing Grace, she probably couldn't be stifled.

So her parents couldn't handle it and they shipped her off to some university where she'd been put to work from the age of eight, conducting research and writing papers that would bring acclaim and new funding for the university. But it sounded like she'd never been allowed to have a life outside of the school. She'd certainly never had a boyfriend, or she wouldn't have still been a virgin. On the other hand, she didn't seem unhappy with her life. In fact, she seemed happy, loving, well-adjusted. She got along great with everyone at the resort. So maybe he just needed to stop worrying about it.

"Ready to come about," he shouted, and watched Grace scramble to get out of the way of the boom, then pull the mainsheet taut as he'd showed her.

"Good job, mate," he called out.

She laughed. "Thanks, Captain."

Once the boat was on course, Grace moved aft and sat with him on the small padded bench where he showed her how to steer and steady the wheel.

"You're a natural," he said after Grace had been steering the boat for a few minutes.

"I'm just a good student," she said, smiling as she gazed up at the full sail, resplendent against the blue tropical sky.

Logan had to agree. Hell, maybe she really had been better off at school than at home with her parents. Sounded to Logan like they were the real oddballs, not Grace.

Yes, she was really smart, but she was also funny and

sweet. She had a great attitude and enjoyed learning new things. She'd taken to the cocktail waitressing gig as well as any of the other waiters on staff. Okay, she still got a lot of assistance from the others, but that was because they all liked her and didn't want to see her get fired.

He still had to laugh whenever he thought back to their first conversation about the spores. She'd been so adamant about staying on the island, and now he was glad she had. Not that it mattered, of course. She would leave eventually. Logan figured the timing would be just right for him to move on to the next woman anyway. That's how it had always been and it would keep on going that way. Women were a plentiful commodity. And as he and Aidan had always said, the more the merrier.

For now, though, for as long as it lasted, he was more than satisfied to spend his time with Grace.

"It's so beautiful," she said, pointing to the coast.

"Yeah, it is," Logan murmured, then realized he wasn't even looking at the shoreline.

"This chicken salad is delicious," Grace said after taking her first bite.

"The kitchen does a great job with picnics and box lunches," Logan said, as he spooned more coleslaw onto his plate.

They'd dropped anchor in a small deserted inlet a mile beyond the picturesque port town of Tierra del Alleria, and Grace and Logan had unpacked the picnic basket the hotel kitchen had prepared. Along with chicken salad sandwiches, there was orzo salad and Asian-style coleslaw. It was simple food expertly prepared, and Grace's mouth was watering by the time she'd filled her plate. The kitchen staff had also tucked a half bottle of crisp white wine into the basket, along with brownies for dessert.

They ate and talked, and Grace felt a little tug at her heart as she replayed Logan's earlier words when he'd defended her against her parents. Grace no longer blamed her parents for anything they'd done, but it still gave her a warm feeling to know that Logan was on her side.

He and Dee were the first people she'd ever shared her background with, outside the university, and they had both rushed to support her unconditionally. Nobody in her life had ever done that for her before and she felt so much love for them because of it. And of course she'd used the word *love* in the friendliest sense possible. Nothing more. Good grief, she'd known these people for less than two weeks. And yet, she had to admit she felt closer to Logan and Dee and Joey and Clive and some of the others, than she did to the lab colleagues she'd known for years. And what did that say about her life up to now?

"Everything okay, Grace?" Logan asked, rubbing her knee gently. "You look a little anxious all of a sudden."

She gazed at him with what she hoped was a carefree smile. "I'm fine. Wonderful. I was just, um, a little worried that we'll never finish all this food."

He took another big bite of his sandwich and grinned at her. "That's never been a big problem for me."

They napped in the shade of the mainsail, then made love below deck in the well-appointed, mahogany-lined forward cabin where a cool breeze wafted through the open brass portholes. Grace had enjoyed exploring the cleverly arranged space, but all those fun design details drifted into the ether as Grace lost herself in the exquisite sensation of having Logan sheathed inside her.

Pleasure built as he drove into her again. They gazed at each other and Logan's mouth curved in a smile of satisfaction that indicated pure male approval. Then his face shifted, his jaw tightened, his eyes squeezed closed as his breath grew ragged and passion rose to a fever pitch. His murmured endearments awakened her innermost desires and Grace's heart beat even faster as every nerve ending inside her was stretched to the limit. Then in an instant, they all flew free in an explosion of joy more colorful than any Fourth of July celebration she'd ever experienced.

Seconds later, waves of tension rippled through him and he cried out her name, then joined her in this place that was beyond anywhere she'd ever been before.

A while later, he gathered her in his arms and dozed for a time. His pounding heart grew quiet and steady against her chest and she felt completely cherished for the first time in her life. If they never left the boat again, she knew she could be perfectly happy here. Then her eyes fluttered open and she gazed up at his expression. Maybe she was dreaming, but she would've sworn she was looking into the face of serenity, pure and simple.

And that's when she knew she was in big trouble.

It was early afternoon the following day when Grace glanced around at the fertile hillside of palm trees and couldn't believe her amazing good luck. Fumbling in her bag for her forceps, she kept her focus on the profusion of spore-rich fronds she'd just discovered. The groupings looked slightly thicker and darker than the others down in the palmetto grove. Was that due simply to the lack of direct sunlight on the hill or were these new spores a different subspecies? Would these more prolific creatures provide even more insight into the scientific puzzle she was on the verge of solving? She could only hope and pray that they would.

She'd spent the morning collecting samples from the palmetto trees. Then, on a hunch, she'd walked a few hundred yards along the trail that led into the rain forest, stopping when she reached a fork. Instead of the wider trail she'd taken before, she chose the narrow, less worn path that clung to the side of the rugged green hill and meandered even farther into the vast canopy of verdant trees, thick vines and wild green ferns.

It was hot and close, with sunlight only managing to peek through the heavy trees occasionally. The thick scents of the rain forest wrapped themselves around her and she smiled despite the sweat she felt rolling along her spine.

The path continued climbing up and around one hill to another area of the forest where she found more palm trees growing in scattered profusion up and down the hillside. She stopped to study the fronds at the base of one tree that grew close enough to the path, since she didn't dare veer off in her lightweight sandals. Next time she decided to hike into the hills, she would wear appropriate shoes.

After collecting as many spores as her forceps would grab, she stacked her petri dishes in her bag and looked around at her surroundings.

With a short laugh, she realized that after walking for at least an hour, she'd barely risen thirty or forty feet above the forest floor. But the view was incomparable anyway. From here she could see a slice of coastline in the distance. Unlike the calm, protected waters of Logan's bay, there were waves swelling and tumbling onto that faraway beach. Did Logan ever go surfing there?

She turned and stared at the tops of the trees and felt tears sting her eyes. That's when she hugged herself, knowing she'd never seen a view more exotically beautiful in her life. After a few minutes, she pulled out her smartphone and took some pictures, despite knowing they could never convey the true colors and natural splendor of the real thing. That was okay. The photos would at least provide a reminder to Grace that she had, indeed, stood in this place once upon a time.

A movement caught her eye and she glanced to the nearest hill across the expanse of trees. A narrow rush of water fell over rocks and shrubs on its way down the hill and formed a waterfall that splashed into a small, secluded pool at the base.

Surrounded by thick plants and greenery, the tiny pool wasn't visible at first. But now she could barely wait to see it up close. She wondered if Logan knew it was here. Then she wondered if he would come back here with her. She shivered at the thought of the two of them frolicking in their own private lagoon.

Her next thought caused her to shiver again, and not in a good way. Were there alligators? Snakes? She would have to find out for certain before she dared step foot in the water.

"What would paradise be without a snake?" she muttered aloud, and shivered all over again. But it was too lovely a day to be harboring sucky thoughts of reptiles, so with a mental shove, she rid her mind of all images of slithery creatures. Instead, she went with the much more pleasant daydream of lazing the day away with Logan in their own private rain forest swimming pool. As she picked up her kit and headed out of the forest, she smiled in anticipation.

Seven

Logan stood beside the limousine and watched Aidan jog down the stairs of the brothers' Gulfstream G650 jet before strolling across the tarmac. He was followed closely by their Senior VP, Eleanor, and two corporate staffers as a crew of airport workers began unloading luggage from the plane onto a cart.

"Welcome home, bro," Logan said, and grabbed his brother in a bear hug. Then he shook hands with Eleanor and the two staffers. "You all did a great job in New York. Thanks."

They all piled into the limo and while they waited for their luggage to be loaded into the trunk, Logan passed around bottles of beer to anyone who wanted one. He knew he did. He'd spent the past two hours dealing with Pierre, his irate hotel manager, and the entire housekeeping staff, who were in various stages of tears and anguish after Pierre had reamed them for stealing from a hotel guest.

Nobody had confessed and Pierre was on the verge of firing every one of them. But armed combat was unexpectedly averted when the hotel guest called Logan's office to announce that, oops, she'd found her diamond necklace after all, in another handbag she'd forgotten she brought.

Pierre was still simmering and the staff were all nursing grudges that would eventually fade. Pierre tended to hit pretty high on the drama meter, but he was also savvy enough to make it up to the staffers for insinuating there was a thief among them. They were all used to Pierre's over-the-top reactions, but the fact that he cared so very much about the guests' safety and comfort was what made him an excellent manager.

Still, that was the last time Logan would ever make the mistake of casually asking the hotel manager how things were going.

After the short drive back to the hotel, Logan and Aidan waved off the staffers and headed for Aidan's suite.

While his brother changed from a business suit into a pair of cargo shorts and a T-shirt, Logan pulled two more bottles of beer out of the refrigerator, opened them and handed one to his brother.

"Thanks," Aidan said, and took a long drink. "Damn, feels like I've been gone a month."

Logan sat in an overstuffed chair and rested the beer bottle on his knee. "And to me, it's as if you'd barely left."

"Ah, feel the love," Aidan said, laughing. The two brothers grinned at each other, staring into identical blue eyes that reflected the exact same image back at them.

They had grown up so identical that no one besides their father had ever been able to tell them apart. Even close friends and family members, people who should've been able to tell the difference, couldn't. Their mother, for instance, had always mixed them up, from the time they were born. But then, she'd never really bothered to get to know them. And when she disappeared when the twins were seven, no one was too surprised.

Ancient history, Logan thought, and shook off the grim memory. Aidan wanted an update on anything new that was happening at the hotel and Logan brought him up to date on each department.

As he spoke about the latest housekeeping kerfuffle and filled his brother in on new staffing and such, Aidan unpacked. He made several piles of laundry on the bed, then put in a call to housekeeping.

"Tomorrow after the conference call, we need to finalize the Dukes' visit," Logan said as soon as Aidan was off the phone.

"Good thinking." Aidan found his briefcase and pulled out a thick, leather-bound notepad. "I've made some notes."

Logan still couldn't quite believe he and his brother had never met their Duke cousins until this past year. Adam, Brandon and Cameron Duke were the adopted sons of Sally Duke, who was the widow of the twins' father's brother, William.

Logan grinned. The convoluted nature of their relationship confused him sometimes, too.

But a year ago, Logan's father, Tom, had received a call out of the blue from Sally Duke, explaining the connection.

Brothers William and Tom had lost their parents in a car crash and been sent to live in an orphanage in San Francisco for a few years until William was adopted. In those days, there was no concern for keeping siblings together, so the boys never saw each other again.

Once he was old enough, William tried to contact the orphanage to find his brother, but the place had burned to the ground five years earlier and all the records had been lost.

Sally had picked up the lost trail after William died and spent years trying to track down Tom. Thanks to the miracle of internet search engines, she finally found him, along with his two boys who were now grown men. Sally had arranged for a family reunion and now they all tried to get together as often as possible. And it seemed to Logan that their father might've developed a bit of a crush on Sally.

Since the Duke brothers built hotels, it had been a natural move for Logan and Aidan to eventually invite them to Alleria to see if they might be interested in expanding their empire to the Caribbean.

They'd be here next weekend, and Logan and Aidan intended to pull out all the stops and show them the best that Alleria had to offer. And thinking about that, Logan was reminded that he really needed to show Grace the hot springs in the rain forest.

Putting thoughts of a wet, naked Grace out of his mind, Logan watched his brother move around the room putting his things away. In that moment, Logan realized that a part of him felt much more relaxed now that Aidan was back on the island. It was almost as if he'd been missing a body part or something. It was no big deal, just another weird twin phenomenon he and Aidan had laughed about their entire lives.

"You want to go for Mexican food?" Aidan asked.

"How'd you know?"

Aidan just grinned as he used his foot to straighten the line of shoes in his closet.

Logan lined his shoes like that, too, he thought, and added the quirk to the list of oddities that went along with being a twin. Although, watching Aidan go down the line of shoes again, nudging them minutely, he wondered if this particular quirk wasn't more like a case of mutual OCD.

He finished his beer and tossed the empty bottle into the recycling can. "Let's go."

After returning from the rain forest, Grace had tried to track down Logan to tell him about the temptingly secluded pool she'd seen and what she'd like to do about it with him. But one of the clerks had told her he'd gone to the airport to pick up his brother, so she went to her room instead and had been studying spores ever since.

At least, she'd tried to study the spores when thoughts of Logan weren't interfering. She wondered if she would see him in the lounge tonight. Would he introduce her to his brother, Aidan? Would Aidan like her? She hoped so. She knew that the two men were twins. Everyone on the staff talked about them, especially the women. Apparently, it was impossible to tell them apart.

That's when another thought suddenly interfered: How would Grace know which one was Logan? Would she embarrass herself in front of his brother?

She couldn't imagine not being able to tell the difference between the man she'd spent so many hours laughing and talking and making love with, and his brother. What kind of woman would that make her?

She couldn't wrap her mind around that possibility, so she forced herself to concentrate on her work. She'd studied slide after slide of the new spores and under the microscope, these new batches appeared to have the exact same qualities as the original group. But time—and her ultrapowerful electron microscope back in the laboratory—would tell.

She jolted when the buzzer on her travel alarm went off. She pressed the off button, then closed up her notepad and

began to prepare to take a hot shower before heading out
to her evening job in the cocktail lounge.

Removing her clothes, she folded them on top of her
bed, then walked into the bathroom. A sudden image of
Logan standing in the shower with her, his broad chest
glistening with soapy water, brought a shiver to her spine
and a smile to her face as she waited for the water to get
hot.

"At this rate, you'll need a *cold* shower," she told her
reflection in the rapidly fogging mirror, then stepped into
the shower stall.

As she washed and rinsed her hair, Grace's thoughts
drifted back to Logan's reaction at finding out how smart
she was. Most men she'd known would've brushed her
off. For goodness' sake, if she was being honest about
it, even her own father and mother had brushed her off.
But Logan seemed to enjoy the fact that she was knowl-
edgeable, that she paid attention and enjoyed learning new
things. It was heartening that he seemed to like her and to
want her to stay with him, because the feeling was mutual.
She'd never wanted anything quite as badly as she wanted
him. Even temporarily, which was all she could really hope
for anyway.

She'd given up trying to lecture herself on falling in
love with him since she was pretty sure it was too late.
Maybe she should've tried a little harder; because, after
all, in case she needed to be reminded, she really couldn't
be trusted when it came to her feelings for men. Remember Walter.

But as she rinsed her hair one last time, she realized
that she couldn't exactly recall Walter's face. How odd
was that? It would be wonderful if Walter and his face
were truly just a vague memory now. If she was lucky, she
would never have to see the man again.

Logan was another matter altogether. His face was etched in her memory so clearly, she was pretty certain she would never forget him. Still, she thought it might be nice to ask Dee to take a surreptitious photograph of Grace standing next to Logan. It would be lovely to have something to look at and remember him by. But even if she couldn't get a picture, she would never forget his face. Or his body. Or his voice. Or his kiss.

She really would need that cold shower at this rate.

Turning off the water, she grabbed a towel and dried off. She couldn't help it if her thoughts continually turned to Logan. He was simply the loveliest man she'd ever known and part of her wished, foolishly, that she would never have to leave Alleria.

Her more practical mind argued that nothing lasted forever. Even if she stayed on the island, Logan might very well grow tired of her. And what would happen then? Would he fire her? Or would he just make it so impossible for her to be happy here that she would end up leaving anyway?

That thought was such an unhappy one that it left an achy feeling in her chest. She absently rubbed her sternum to ease the pain as she told herself firmly that it was better all the way around to leave when she planned. Before Logan began to look at her with boredom, or, worse… irritation in his eyes.

Shaking off the heaviness around her heart, she applied a touch of mascara and lip gloss, then walked over to the dresser and pulled out the bikini and sarong that made up her uniform. And since she was standing by the dresser anyway, she checked the microscope slide again.

Then she checked it one more time.

"That can't be right," she said. She rechecked her notes. Had she made a mistake in notating the circumference around the edges of the new spore gathering? She didn't think she had, so she looked back at the slide. Then her notes.

Either she was seeing things, or the spores were replicating at least three times faster than the ones back in the lab at the university. If it was true, if she wasn't hallucinating, then these new spores from the top of the rain forest were stronger, faster and more efficient than any she'd found before.

She did a little happy dance. It was an unexpected breakthrough, a development she couldn't have foreseen in a million years. She should've been itching to get back to the laboratory and the more precise equipment she could use to measure things more accurately. But all she wanted to do was track down Logan and share her news with him. After all, it was Logan who'd allowed her to stay on the island, thus providing her with the opportunity to find these spores and accelerate her experimentation. She thought it only fair that she thank him for that.

Her face heated up as she considered the many inventive ways she could show him how grateful she was.

Lively mariachi music floated out to the patio of Casa Del Puerto, where Aidan and Logan sat enjoying the three items the restaurant was most famous for: fajitas, homemade tortillas and an unsurpassed view of the picturesque harbor of Tierra del Alleria. The margaritas weren't bad, either.

The quaint Tierra marina was where Logan and Aidan had first docked their boat on their original visit to Alleria. They'd needed to have their boat overhauled and intended to stay a week while the work was done. It had never crossed their minds to buy land here, least of all the entire island.

But when the week was over and their sailboat was ready, they decided to stay another week, slowly falling in love with the sleepy harbor town, its charming residents, miles of white-sand beaches and an amazing rain forest.

They learned during that visit that one of the smaller cruise lines featuring sailing yachts had recently negotiated to add Tierra to its itinerary. The brothers recognized that the island was on its way to becoming a key Caribbean destination within a few years. They made an appointment with the major landowner on the island about buying property and that's when they found out that the island itself was up for sale.

The brothers had survived on their gut instincts long enough to have a sixth sense for knowing when something sounded right. They spoke to their fledgling investor group and within two months they were the proud owners of their very own Caribbean island. Once the ink on the contracts was dry, the first order of business had been the design and construction of a luxury resort that would truly establish Alleria as a premier destination for the most discerning travelers in the world.

Now, seven years later, that goal had been met, and the hotel also served as the corporate headquarters for all the Sutherland enterprises. They had offices in New York and San Francisco, as well; but Alleria was the home as well as the heart of their operations.

Logan smeared a fresh tortilla with a hearty spoonful of refried beans and a healthy dab of hot sauce, then wrapped it up and bit into a little taste of heaven.

Aidan sat back in his chair, patting his stomach. "That's it for me."

"I'll be done after this last bite," Logan admitted.

"Good," Aidan said. "Then we can talk."

"We've been talking all night," Logan said, gazing at his brother with suspicion as he took a sip of his drink.

"Yeah, but, funny thing, this subject never came up," Aidan said, stretching his legs out to the side of the table. "You see, Ellie was talking to Serena day before yesterday and she mentioned a certain new cocktail waitress you've been spending time with."

It was a good thing Logan had swallowed his margarita or he would've spewed it all over the table. And that would've been a waste of good alcohol. His eyes narrowed on his brother. "So now you're listening to employee gossip?"

Aidan shrugged. "When the source of the gossip comes from the management level, I'm willing to pay attention."

Just his luck, Logan thought. Serena was manager of catering which included the cocktail lounge and the various restaurants throughout the hotel. And Ellie was one of her best friends. "So what's the problem?"

"Dude, you're dating an employee?" Aidan said. "Are you out of your mind?"

"She's not really an employee."

Aidan snorted. "Interesting that you'd say that since she's on the payroll. And, according to Serena, she actually does work in the cocktail lounge. Sounds like an employee to me."

"*Temporary* employee," Logan said.

One wary eyebrow shot up. "What's that supposed to mean?"

Logan pushed his plate away and sat back in his chair. It had only been a matter of time before the subject of Grace came up, so he figured he'd better deal with it here and now and put a stop to the gossip.

He explained to Aidan how the new cocktail waitress had come to the island under false pretenses and how he'd fired her, then spelled out the circumstances under which he'd allowed her to stay on.

"Okay." Aidan nodded agreeably. "I get how she arrived and I'm willing to go along with her staying, if you think it's justified."

"It is."

"But I haven't heard how all that turned into you *dating* her."

"Because she's…"

Aidan leaned forward. "Sorry? I didn't catch that. What'd you say?"

Logan scowled. "None of your damn business."

"Ah." Aidan nodded, his mouth twisting in a grin. "So she's hot."

"Shut up."

Aidan chuckled. "I'll take that as a yes." His smile faded and he said, "Look, when we talked the other day, I heard something in your voice I don't remember hearing before. So sue me for being concerned."

"Nothing to be concerned about."

Aidan studied him for another long moment. "I'm not convinced."

"Tough. It doesn't matter anyway. Grace doesn't expect anything from me but great sex. Besides, she'll only be here for another few weeks and then she's leaving."

"You sure she's leaving?"

"Yeah. She's leaving." Saying the words aloud brought a frown to Logan's face. Strange, but he didn't want her to leave just yet. He was still having a good time with her. Why break it off when they were having a good time?

Okay, yeah, Grace was unlike any woman he'd ever known; so, yeah, he could admit he was, well, sort of captivated by her. Who wouldn't be? She was a beautiful woman with an amazing brain and an even more incredible heart. He liked her.

But that's all this was. It wasn't like he *cared* for her. He didn't *care* for any woman. It was just that she was... unique. Funny. Smart. And sexy as hell. They'd been having fun together and that would continue for as long as it lasted. Then she'd go home. Things would be over between them and that would be the end of it. No harm, no foul.

But Aidan had been watching him carefully and now he shook his head in disgust. "Crap, man. You're falling for her."

"What?" Shocked at the idea, Logan snorted a laugh. "That's a load of bull. I'm not falling for her."

"Yeah, you are."

Irritated by his brother's scrutiny, Logan grabbed his margarita and chugged it down. "How stupid do you think I am? I haven't forgotten that she lied and manipulated her way onto the island, so why on earth would I ever trust her, let alone fall for her? So let it go."

"You're sleeping with her."

"So what?"

"You of all people should know how women are." Aidan sat forward with his elbows resting on his knees and shook his head. "Once you're sleeping with them, they think they've got you by the balls. And, damn it, what do you really know about this woman? She comes here under false pretenses with this bizarre story about spores, which is damn strange to begin with, by the way. I mean, really. Spores? Is she into biological warfare or something?"

"They're good spores," Logan muttered.

"Oh, I feel so much better, thanks." Aidan shook his head. "So, anyway, once this woman gets here, she latches onto you faster than a tic on a hound dog and now you're falling for her. How did that happen?"

"I'm not falling for her," Logan repeated through gritted teeth. "It's nothing like that. And seriously? Tic on a hound dog?"

"I just spent two days on the phone with Tex," Aidan said with a shrug. "I've gone country."

"Good to know."

"Okay, now look," Aidan said slowly. "I understand if you have feelings for this girl."

"You don't understand squat."

"No really, there's nothing wrong with that."

"You're completely off base," Logan said. "Just drop it."

But Aidan was on a roll. "I'll drop it as soon as you hear me out. Has it occurred to you that she's after your money?"

Logan barked out a laugh, then laughed harder at the very idea. Grace? A gold digger? Come on. "You're so wrong it's not funny." He relaxed in his chair. "Look, you don't know her, so I'll give you a pass on that. But trust me, it's impossible. She's not like that. Her whole world is wrapped up in her research. You should see her room. She's got a microscope and all this equipment and reams of notes. There's no way she's…"

Aidan continued watching him as Logan mentally replayed a few conversations he'd had with Grace.

"Well?"

Logan shook his head with firm resolve. "Nope. Absolutely not."

"I think you're not looking at her from an objective point of view."

"Duh." Logan glared at his brother. "Just because I'm not being objective doesn't mean I'm some naive idiot, either."

"Fine. Prove it to me, then."

"Yeah? How?"

Aidan smiled and his eyebrows lifted high on his forehead. "Easy enough. I say we need to pull the Switch."

Logan leaned forward and pounded the table with his fist. "No way. Don't even think about it."

Over the years, the brothers had occasionally pulled the Switch on women, usually just for fun or when one of the brothers seemed to be getting too serious about a woman. Aidan had always called it a test, implemented merely to see if a woman was paying attention to which brother was which.

The last time they'd employed the Switch was when Logan suspected that his wife, Tanya, was being less than faithful to their marriage vows. He'd asked Aidan to pull the Switch on her. Tanya didn't pass the test.

"Fine," Aidan said, holding up his hands in surrender. "You win. But I still want to meet her. Let's just swing by the lounge on the way back so you can introduce me to her."

"You're not meeting her."

"You know how stupid you sound?"

Logan clenched his teeth together, then blew out a heavy sigh. "Yeah, I'm pretty clear on that. Fine, we'll swing by, I'll introduce you, you'll say hello, then you'll shut up and leave."

Aidan grinned. "You're not doing yourself any favors here."

"I know," Logan muttered. What was wrong with him? It was no big deal if Aidan met Grace. But there was no way he'd allow his brother to pull the Switch on her.

"So what's her name?"

He hesitated, but his brother's expression switched to

one of such abject *pity,* he finally blurted, "Grace. Her name's Grace."

Aidan smile in satisfaction. "Pretty name. Where's she from?"

Logan rolled his eyes. "Minnesota."

"Ah, a farm girl," his brother murmured.

"No, a scientist," Logan said flatly.

"Oh, right, the spores. Tell me more."

"They're rare spores only found on Alleria. Grace is studying their replication patterns in hope of curing diseases and saving lives someday."

"No kidding?"

"Yeah."

Aidan folded his arms across his chest. "Seems to me you know a hell of a lot about spores all of a sudden."

"Yeah, I do," Logan said, taking a long sip of his drink. "We've got miracle spores on Alleria and I'm swollen with pride over that."

Aidan choked on a laugh. "Damn, it's good to be home."

"I've missed you, too," Logan said dryly.

"Right." Aidan grinned. "You sure you don't want to reconsider the Switch? It's always worked for us before. And wouldn't you rather know the truth for sure?"

Pissed off now, Logan flopped back in his chair. Knowledge was power, even when the truth sucked. Besides, he had more than a sneaking feeling that Aidan would carry out the Switch whether Logan approved or not. And there was the added fact that once Aidan had met Grace and seen how sincere and real she was, he'd back off and leave Logan to enjoy her for the short amount of time he had with her.

"Fine," he said, lifting his margarita glass in a toast.

"Give it your best shot. But if you hurt her, I'll have to kill you."

"Fair enough," Aidan said with a laugh, and called for the check.

Eight

"Hey, babe," he said from close behind her, his tone warm and intimate. "I missed you last night."

Grace whipped around and laughed with joy. "Oh, Logan, I missed you, too. I'm so happy to…" Her voice faded and she smiled curiously as she studied him more carefully.

He'd called her late last night after her shift had ended to let her know he couldn't see her. He'd sounded as disappointed as she'd felt, so Grace hadn't worried too much that he was losing interest or whatever equally foolish scenario she could've dreamed up in the moment.

And now, just knowing that he'd come looking for her this morning and that he knew her well enough to know she'd be walking on the beach toward the palmetto grove, was sweetly heartening.

Would it be too outrageous if she dragged him off to

the shelter of the rain forest and had her way with him? Her body tingled at the thought.

But…something was wrong. Logan wasn't… Hmm. She gazed at him, trying to figure out what was different. Was it his ears? Was it…?

"Babe," he said, his handsome smile fading to a look of concern. He reached out and lightly gripped her upper arm. "Are you all right?"

Yes, she was all right, but he was…different somehow.

"Ah," Grace said slowly and her smile broadened. "You must be Aidan. Hello." She reached out and took his hand in a warm handshake. "How do you do?"

"Babe, that's crazy." He took a half step back. "I'm not—"

"I've often wondered what it would be like to be a twin, especially an identical twin. It must be fascinating to look at another person and see your own face staring back at you." She took her time and circled all the way around him, trailing her hand along his waistline as she examined his posture, the fine laugh lines around his compelling eyes, the shape of his head, the way his chiseled jaw met his strong, square chin. All of it was so appealingly rugged. "Well, it's extraordinary, isn't it? You look exactly like Logan."

"But I *am* Logan," he insisted, scowling now.

"Oh, that's so funny," she said, laughing at his joke as she patted his arm. "I've always found the concept of twins so interesting. You two must've been able to play the best tricks on people."

"We don't play tricks," he ground out as his forehead furrowed in annoyance.

"Really? I certainly would've if I had a twin sister." She sighed at the thought. "We could have practiced smiling the same way—unless you do that anyway? Do you?

I mean, you and Logan of course. Do you instinctively do things in the same manner or was it learned behavior? You know, they do twin studies all the time and identical twins are in high demand. Have either of you ever thought of donating some time to scientific exploration?"

"Scientific…" He sounded confused.

Well, Grace was used to that kind of reaction, but not from Logan, she realized, and that made her smile even brighter.

She threaded her arm through Aidan's and they walked along the shore for a bit before she stopped and squeezed his arm enthusiastically. "You do know that identical twins come from the same egg. Of course you know that. Why wouldn't you? Oh, but what a thrill to imagine the fertile egg separating in the womb. To watch a zygote's first cellular division as it becomes two living beings. What miracle of nature triggers the split? Do you often ask yourself that question? It's incredible on every level, isn't it?"

He stared at her as if she'd sprouted antennae, but again, she was used to that.

"Grace…"

"Oh, it's all right, Aidan. I understand why you would want to play a trick on me! If I had a twin sister, I would want to test her boyfriends, too. In fact, I'm sort of thrilled that the two of you would take the time to plan this out. Makes me feel sort of special, you know?"

"You're not mad?"

"Oh, no, this is fun."

"It was my idea," he muttered.

"Of course it was." She grinned up at him. "I'm just so pleased to meet you. Logan speaks very highly of you, you know."

"He does?"

"Oh, yes."

His eyes narrowed. "Seriously, how do you know I'm not Logan?"

"What a silly question," she said, smiling. "Walk with me, Aidan."

They continued walking companionably and she gazed sideways at his powerfully built chest and muscular shoulders so clearly outlined by his T-shirt. With a sigh, Grace noted that Aidan and Logan Sutherland were simply magnificent-looking men. Staring up at Aidan's handsome face, she smiled again. It was remarkable that he was so identical to his brother, yet, somehow, so very different.

Logan had never called her "babe" before. And despite their first confrontation shortly after she'd broken all those glasses and Logan had appeared so cynical and grim, Grace could see that Aidan had an even more sardonic wit than his brother.

There was more, of course. Though their features were identical, Logan held his head differently. And it might be her imagination, but his mouth quirked a bit higher on one side when he gave her that devastating half smile. And his eyes seemed to shine more brightly. His hair, she thought, looked thicker to her. More…touchable.

And yet, none of that took away from the fact that they were both ridiculously stunning specimens of masculinity.

But Aidan continued to stare at her and his mouth twisted in puzzlement. He stopped walking finally and turned to gaze out at the water as he let go of a heavy sigh.

"Are you all right, Aidan?" she asked, clutching his arm. "You look a little flushed. It might be the heat. You should probably be wearing a hat."

"I'm…fine," he mumbled, pushing his hand through his closely cropped hair. Even their haircuts were identical. "Look, Grace, it's been great meeting you, but I've gotta get back to…you know." He waved his hand in the general direction of the hotel.

"It was so nice meeting you, too, Aidan." She stood on her tiptoes and kissed his cheek. "I hope we can talk again soon."

"Yeah. Soon." And he walked away, still shaking his head.

"Damn it, it's not funny."

But Logan threw his head back and laughed anyway. "She's priceless. She took it down to the zygotes? You gotta love that."

"It's not funny," Aidan repeated emphatically as he paced in front of Logan's wide desk. "Nobody but Dad has ever been able to tell us apart before. I don't know what it means, but it's a cause for concern."

"Grace is just more observant than most people. Cut her some slack." Logan sat back in his office chair and asked the question he'd been stupidly worrying about all morning. "So, did you like her?"

Aidan thought for a moment, then shrugged. "Yeah. She was kind of sweet. And gorgeous, of course, but you knew that already. Damn, those eyes of hers. And that hair color is amazing. Do you think it's real? Wait, I guess you would know the truth."

"That's enough."

Aidan rolled his eyes. "Dude, you're pitiful."

"I'm pitiful? You're the one making rude comments."

"Sorry. But you know, when she first turned around and saw me, she looked at me like she wanted to eat me alive—in the best possible way, just so you know." Aidan scraped his knuckles across his jaw in contemplation. "Of course, she thought I was you at the time. But within seconds she'd busted me. And after that, it was just weird to see her staring at me like I was something she might find under her microscope."

"Hey, it's your own damn fault for trying to trick her. At least she didn't smack you, even though you kind of deserved it."

"Huh," Aidan said, as he studied him. "You're taking her side. What's up with that?"

Logan chuckled. "Anyone who can cause you to flip out this much? I'm on their side."

Aidan's eyes narrowed in thought and he began to pace again. "What if she couldn't really tell us apart, but she's been watching us? You know, like maybe she stalked you this morning. You keep your window wide-open half the time. Maybe she saw you in the business suit and knew as soon as I showed up in khakis that I wasn't you."

"You know what? You're losing it."

"Yeah, maybe." Aidan sighed. "But what can I say? It was weird."

Logan laughed again. "You're an idiot."

"No, you're an idiot," Aidan said. "Because you really like her."

"I do like the way she took you down a notch."

"Yeah. I guess it was probably funny from a strictly objective point of view." Aidan stopped in midpace and turned. "But what are we going to do about her?"

"*We* aren't going to do anything about her."

"I'm only thinking of you, bro," Aidan said. "She could still be a stalker."

"The fact that Grace was too perceptive to fall for the Switch doesn't make her a stalker." Logan laughed at that ludicrous thought. "Just let it go, man."

"Okay." Aidan slumped down into the visitor's chair. "But I never thought I'd see the day when the Switch would fail me."

"It's a sad day, all right." Logan shook his head, pulled a file out of the credenza and spread it open on his desk. "We need to get this meeting started. I'll buzz Ellie to let her know we're ready to go."

"You promise there are no snakes?"

"Cross my heart." Logan grabbed her hand as the path widened and they were able to walk hand in hand. "We don't have poisonous snakes on Alleria. Yes, we have little green-and-brown snakes that eat bugs and stuff, but that's it. We have a very nonconfrontational ecosystem here on the island."

Grace's eyes widened and she laughed. "Really? Non-confrontational ecosystem? That's so impressive."

"I sound like a science geek, don't I?"

"Yes." Grace sniffled. "I'm so proud."

They both laughed as Logan grabbed her and swung her into his arms. "Come on."

Clouds flitted across the blue sky as they followed the narrowing path that switched back and forth around the hills through the forested area. They found the hot springs twenty minutes later, after cutting their way through the thick fronds and giant leaves of the banana trees that grew close to the source of the thermal heat.

They stopped at the edge of a small pool that had been carved over the centuries into the base of the rock-covered hill. Hot bubbles rose to the surface from the thermal pockets while cool water cascaded down over smooth boulders and splashed into the clear water.

Thick vegetation grew in abundance under the canopy of the rain forest, assuring them of utter privacy.

"It's like our own private paradise," she said, and gazed at him. "Can we go in?"

"Absolutely." Logan stripped off his T-shirt, then pointed

up at the waterfall. "Just so you know, the water coming from the hill is much cooler than the springs itself, so don't be shocked to find pockets of cold mixed in with the hot once you step in."

"So the cold spots aren't from the alligators swishing their tails underwater?"

He bit back a grin. "No alligators."

"I'm trusting you," she said, shaking her finger at him. "I have a deep-seated fear of alligators."

"You and me both, sweetheart." Logan stepped to the edge of the pool. "And I swear the only predatory beasts are the small lizards who only want to sun themselves down in the flatlands."

"Okay. Is the water shallow?" she asked.

"No, it's more like five or six feet deep."

She slipped out of her hiking shorts, then adjusted the strap of her bathing suit where it wrapped around her neck.

Logan, being a mere human, slid his gaze down to her breasts, where the strap adjustment caused them both to lift in a sensual movement that was surely meant to search and destroy every last one of his brain cells.

When her nipples suddenly perked up at his scrutiny, he grinned. Always nice to know the attraction wasn't one-sided.

With little blood left to nourish his brain, Logan was helpless to prevent his gaze from traveling farther down her well-shaped torso, taking in her nicely toned stomach, perfectly rounded hips and long, lovely legs.

When he finally realized that she was watching him as he took his little side trip, Logan forced himself to make eye contact once again.

Sure enough, Grace glared back at him with eyes narrowed and hands pressed to her hips in a mock display of insulted dignity.

"Hey, I'm just a guy," Logan said, laughing. "An uncouth clod of a guy, for sure, but still a guy."

"Have you seen enough?" she demanded to know.

"Not nearly."

Grace smiled. "Maybe you'll get a chance to see more if you behave."

"Not a chance you'll get me to behave out here."

"Well, then." Grace whipped around toward the water. "Last one in the pool is a dirty rotten protozoan."

She jumped into the pool and Logan followed her, creating a riot of waves and splashes as they surfaced. They grabbed blindly for each other and once he had her in his arms, Logan kissed her slowly, deeply, wrapping his tongue around hers as all his pent-up fervor began to unfurl.

In unspoken synchronicity, they began to peel off what little clothing they wore. Logan flung his trunks and her bikini onto the nearest rock, then, despite an aching yearning to be inside her, he turned all of his attention to first satisfying her completely. He was determined to move unhurriedly, though she was so damn tempting with her lovely breasts cresting on the surface of the water.

With both hands on her face, he kissed her again. When she swept her tongue along his lower lip in a move that was both innocent and seductive, his mind emptied of all thought but pleasure, pure and unadulterated.

He took his time with her, working his hands along the sides of her breasts, teasing her nipples to fullness, then moving down her firm stomach to the apex of her thighs where he stroked her soft folds until he heard her blissful sigh. The sweet sound brought his erection instantly to attention and he groaned with desire for her. She reached down and stroked his rigid length until he had to pull away or fall apart in her hands.

Gripping her behind, he squeezed and kneaded lightly as he moved his mouth to cover hers, kissing her long and hard as he continued to touch her all over.

"I need you, Logan," she murmured, and stretched her arms around his neck. "Please."

"I just have to do this first," he whispered, cupping her breasts in his hands, then bending to taste first one, then the other, taking his time to enjoy her soft fullness. "Now wrap your legs around me, sweetheart."

She did as he asked, her breasts pressing against his chest, driving him to madness as he eased her down onto him, then held his breath when she drew him in to the hilt.

Her eyes fluttered closed as passion overcame them both. Logan began to move inside her, thrusting faster and harder, plunging deeper, then deeper still. She cried out her pleasure as she moved with him. Her heated need threatened to drive him to completion too quickly, so he willed himself to go slowly, carefully, dragging each second out as he stroked her innermost core.

But need consumed him once more and pure instinct took over. His movements grew faster, deeper, more frantic as his body pulsated within hers. She screamed his name and moments later, he groaned in response as a wild rapture overtook him and he plunged with her over the edge.

Spent and sated, they lay sprawled on one of the smooth boulders that lined the edge of the pool.

"You're right—this is paradise," Logan said, touching her cheek with his fingers. Then he rolled up onto his elbow and leaned over to kiss her.

She stared at his long, powerful body lying next to her, aching to touch him again. She just wasn't sure she had the strength to move a muscle.

They dozed for a few minutes, then slid into the water

again. She swam toward the waterfall, needing the coolness to quench the heat she felt inside her body and out.

He came and stood behind her and let the water cool them both. He smoothed her hair back with his hands. Then she turned and he pulled her into his arms, holding her against his chest, his solid strength a counterpoint to her soft roundness. She ran her hands along his shoulders and down his back, marveling at the silky smoothness of his skin against the solid firmness of his muscles.

Paradise. Against all odds, she'd found it. And her heart stuttered, knowing it was only a matter of time before she would have to leave it forever.

Two days later, the twins' father, Tom, arrived with Sally Duke and the three Duke brothers and their wives.

The limousine picked all eight of them up at the airport and delivered them back to the hotel in time to get checked in, then meet Logan and Aidan in the cocktail lounge for drinks before dinner.

As they toasted the cousins' arrival with various cocktails and fruit drinks, Logan spied Grace working at the bar.

She should be sitting here with me and my family, he thought. The realization caused him to jolt. Had he really been thinking that? No. He brushed the thought away. Grace wasn't a part of his family. She just worked here. Yes, they were sleeping together. And, yes, he liked her. But, damn, he needed to get real.

Not that it mattered, but Aidan would never let him live it down if he ever found out what Logan had been thinking.

"You must get the cream of the crop in terms of workers," Adam said, glancing around the well-appointed, wide-open room.

"I was just thinking the same thing," his wife, Trish, said. "Your employees are all such beautiful people, and so accommodating."

Brandon's wife Kelly smiled. "And who wouldn't want to work in a tropical paradise?"

"It really is a spectacular location," Sally said, pointing toward the wide wall of windows. "I love this view."

Julia, Cameron's wife, glanced around, then directed a playful scowl at Logan. "So is everyone on your staff required to be gorgeous?"

Everyone at the table laughed, and Logan said, "I've never considered that a job requirement. But I will point out that serving cocktails and food requires the servers to be on their feet for hours while lifting heavy trays the entire time."

"You've got to have great upper-body strength for that job," Brandon said.

"Which means they're all in excellent shape to boot," Kelly said, and laughed despite her look of dismay.

"Besides being so pretty," Sally added.

Logan glanced at Aidan, then gazed around the room and realized it was true. They had a darn good-looking group of people working here. Why hadn't they ever discussed that fact? Maybe they could feature it in one of their online newsletters.

Aidan bit back a grin. "Contrary to every human resources dictate ever written, we have a very strict Pretty People policy here at the Alleria Resort."

"Yeah, right," Logan said, rolling his eyes. "He's kidding. Our Senior Vice President and most of our managers would have our heads if that were true."

"Well, the hotel is beautiful," Sally said, sipping her piña colada. "And everyone has been more than helpful."

"I'm glad," Logan said.

"I can't wait to swim in that clear turquoise water," Julia said dreamily.

"I'm starting with a massage first thing tomorrow," Sally said, then sighed. "All my beautiful grandbabies are taking a toll on my muscles."

"Oh, I'll join you," Kelly said, rubbing her neck. "I'm pretty sure my shoulder was yanked out of its socket when I lifted Robbie yesterday."

"I know what you mean, sweetie." Sally cast a wary glance at Brandon. "I'm afraid that little guy is going to grow up to be a linebacker."

Brandon grinned. "That's my boy."

"I was hoping to get a golf game in first thing," Tom said as he grabbed a chip full of guacamole.

"I'll be glad to join you," Adam said.

"Me, too," Brandon chimed in. "And Kelly's no slacker on the golf course, either."

"Massage first," Kelly said. "But I'd love to play golf the next day."

"I'll go swimming with you, baby," Cameron said, wrapping his arm around Julia's shoulder. With a smile, she closed her eyes and rested her head on his chest.

Logan felt a tug of envy at his cousins' good luck at finding three such beautiful, accomplished women to marry. He knew they each had one or two really cute kids, too. So they'd clearly never had a qualm about trusting a woman enough to marry and settle down with her. Of course, they'd grown up with Sally, who was a fantastic mom and must've provided them with a happy home despite her husband's untimely death. The Duke brothers had never known a mother's betrayal or experienced the treachery of a manipulative, lying woman.

Lucky dogs.

* * *

Logan wiped away the sweat from his eyes as he ran to the end of the peninsula and rounded the slow curve of white-blond sand. He headed back toward the hotel, his heart pounding in rhythm with his feet. He observed a few others out this morning, running or walking to the beat of the music blasting into their heads through tiny earbuds.

He tried to concentrate exclusively on his breathing, but the thought of Grace's lush, naked body still warming his bed caused his body to tighten. It had seemed like a good idea to force himself to get up and go running this morning, but now he couldn't quite figure out why.

Pacing himself, he marked time and distance as he passed the familiar landmarks of life here on Alleria. The paddle tennis courts where he and his brother took turns beating each other. The grassy pavilion where concerts were held during the high season. The tiny marina where the hotel kept a fleet of sleek catamarans for guests to rent and where the brothers docked their sailboat.

Thinking of the sailboat reminded him of Grace and their recent picnic. And her lush, naked body.

"Damn," he muttered, and tried to focus on the sound of his shoes pounding against the damp, hard-packed sand. The bay water smelled briny this morning and he wondered if the local fishermen might be reeling in more bluefish in the near future.

The colors of the sunrise were muted pink and coral and so rich it almost hurt to gaze at the swirling hues. He would never admit to a single soul that it was those colors and the island scents that brought him out here at this absurdly early hour of the morning. Exercise was simply an excuse.

"Hey, cousin," a voice called out.

Logan turned and saw Brandon Duke running toward

him and slowed his pace. "Morning, Brandon. You're up early."

"Couldn't sleep," Brandon said, then shook his head. "Don't laugh, but I miss my kid."

"I'm not laughing. That's nice to hear."

Brandon turned and headed back to the hotel with Logan. "Kelly tells me I'm crazy and that it's good to get away for a few days. But she misses him, too. I caught her staring at all of his pictures on her phone."

"How old is he now?"

"Just seven months," Brandon said. "Doesn't seem right to just leave him with the nanny, does it? But here we are."

"You got pictures?"

"Aw, jeez, don't ask. I've got a phone loaded with his photos, too. And I'm willing to bore—I mean, share them with anyone foolish enough to ask."

Logan laughed. "You're a good dad."

"Yeah," Brandon said, shaking his head in wonder. "Who would've thought."

"Well, you had a great mom growing up to show you how it's done."

"Not exactly," Brandon said, grimacing.

"What do you mean?" Logan asked.

"We all came from different screwed-up families and landed in the foster system around the same time," he explained. "Sally adopted the three of us when we were all about eight years old."

Logan stared at him. "I didn't know that."

"Yeah. Before that fateful day, I'd spent eight years living with a crack addict mother and a subhuman piece of crap I hesitate to call a father. He beat the hell out of us from the first moment I could remember. After a few hundred brutal beatings, dear old mom hit the road, leaving me alone with the monster. Luckily, a good neighbor turned him in to child services and I ended up in foster care. But I never forgot the lessons his fists taught me. Adam and Cameron had similar experiences. We're all damn lucky Sally found us."

Logan stopped walking. Troubled, he glanced around the shore, gazed at the hotel in the distance, then looked back at his cousin. "I...I don't know what to say. Last night I was thinking you and your brothers were the luckiest guys on earth for getting to grow up with a mom like Sally. I was feeling sorry for myself, comparing my life to yours. I figured you guys didn't have a care in the world. Guess I didn't know what I was thinking."

"That's okay," Brandon said. "Sally really did change everything for us. And I *am* the luckiest guy on earth. But it took a few drop kicks from Sally to get me to realize that."

"Yeah? What happened?"

"I was ready to walk away from Kelly."

Logan frowned. "But you two seem perfect for each other."

Brandon grinned as they began to walk again. "Don't get me wrong. I was crazy in love with her and she loved me, too, in spite of the fact that I was a complete knucklehead for thinking I wasn't good enough for her. My thing always was, I didn't want to get close to anyone in case I came up short, you know? Sally's the one who finally smacked some sense into me."

Logan shook his head, pulled a hand towel from his back pocket and wiped more sweat away. "So let me get this straight. You weren't going to marry Kelly because you figured your parents had screwed you up so much that you could never be a decent husband and father?"

"That about covers it."

Logan nodded grimly. He knew Brandon had spent years

in the NFL as a star quarterback, then worked in broadcasting before joining his brothers in their multimillion-dollar business. He defined the word *successful*. Besides that, he was smart, had a great sense of humor and loved his family. The guy was a virtual paragon.

But he'd grown up thinking he was all screwed up?

And now he was well-adjusted and secure enough to admit the mistakes he'd made? Logan was starting to view his cousin in a whole new light.

Through gritted teeth, Logan said, "Our mom walked out on us when we were kids."

"Damn," Brandon said, shaking his head. "Some people are just not meant to have children."

"No kidding."

"But look on the bright side." Brandon chuckled. "At least she did you the favor of leaving you in the hands of a great father."

"That's true." Logan hadn't thought about it from that angle. And now he couldn't help but picture Brandon as the kid who'd been used as a punching bag by a vicious man who never should've been allowed to be a father. But he'd survived. No, he'd more than survived. Brandon had thrived. Logan couldn't help but admire the man he'd become.

He shook his head slowly as he realized he'd completely misjudged his cousins. He was also a little stunned to admit that because of his mother, he'd spent most of his life carrying a chip on his shoulder where women were concerned. Now, after talking to Brandon, he was almost glad she'd left them.

"Damn," he said. "I've been an idiot."

Brandon laughed and slapped his cousin's shoulder companionably. "Welcome to my world, dude."

Nine

"It takes less than two hours to circumnavigate the island," Logan told his cousins after instructing their driver to take the main highway that looped around Alleria. "But that's with no stopping."

"We'll be making four stops, right?" Brandon said, paging through the detailed itinerary Logan's assistant had typed up.

"That's right," Aidan said. "Three possible hotel sites and the proposed sports-center site. Then we'll stop for lunch in Tierra before heading back to our hotel."

Adam put his arm around his wife, who sat next to him in the spacious limousine. "Glad you ladies decided to come with us."

"Me, too," Trish said, glancing around at the other wives. "We can get massages anytime, right? This is much more interesting."

"We like to think so," Aidan said with a grin.

"If you're on the lookout," Logan said, pointing out the window that faced the coast, "you'll be able to see water most of the time."

"Sometimes the growth gets too heavy to see through," Aidan said, "but we're still only within a few hundred yards of the shore at all times."

"That's so cool," Kelly said.

"It's a really small island," Aidan said. "But that's part of its charm."

The first two stops were brief. Everyone agreed that neither of the locations were ideal for the type of hotel that the Dukes specialized in.

"We've got one more spot to look at," Logan said as they continued driving north.

When the limo stopped a few miles later, everyone stared in hushed silence.

"It's perfect," Trish whispered before they'd even climbed out of the limousine. The driver had maneuvered the car down a narrow dirt road and pulled to a stop at the bottom of a rugged hill, inches from the edge of the sandy beach. Tropical palm trees lined the shore and swayed in the soft breeze.

Once they were out of the car and walking around, Kelly pointed in amazement at the hillside above them where flowering vines of every color, shade and variety cascaded down the fertile green surface.

"It's like a painting," she cried, then turned to Brandon. "Isn't it beautiful?"

"Fantastic," he said, pulling her close to him.

"It's incredible," Trish agreed.

Logan had always enjoyed this tranquil cove with its flowering cliffs and wondered why he hadn't brought Grace here before. Someday soon he would take her for a drive and show her the beauty of his island.

As he listened to his cousins and their wives, Logan had every confidence that the Dukes would build the perfect small hotel here that would blend in with the beauty of the land and the sea. He wondered if Grace might come back to visit sometime and see the completed project.

He quickly shook his head, wondering where that thought had come from. Once Grace left, she wouldn't be coming back to visit the island unless she needed more spores. It would be smart for him to keep that in mind.

Julia wandered closer to the water, then turned. "Can I live here?"

Cameron laughed, then said to the others, "This beach is perfect."

"It's on a slight inlet," Aidan explained, pointing to the land that extended out on both sides of the water. "So you're protected from the stronger trade winds. But you've still got more waves coming in than we have on the other side of the island. And there's a nice breeze, so you'll attract a good sailing crowd."

"As long as they bring their money along, we're happy to have them," Adam said with a laugh, always the businessman.

They spent almost an hour exploring the area. They checked the shallow cliffs for erosion and found none. The twins had already commissioned an environmental-impact study and a geological-viability assessment of the land itself. Adam asked how fast and high the tide came in and Aidan had an answer for him.

"But we don't expect you to go by our word alone," Aidan added. "We welcome your independent surveyors and inspection crews."

"Dude," Brandon said, "first of all, you're family, so we're not worried. But, also, you're part of our investment group, so you've got skin in the game, too."

Logan flashed a grin at his brother, then looked at his cousins. "The truth is, we would be building our own hotel here if you hadn't been interested."

"We're interested," Adam said, then glanced at his brothers. "Am I right?"

Cameron and Brandon answered with firm nods, then Cameron said, "Let's have the bean counters work the numbers and we'll draw up the papers."

After a brief stop at the proposed site of the sports center, they had lunch outside on the patio of a small, friendly French bistro that specialized in local fish and shellfish. A colorful market umbrella protected the entire party from the rays of the sun as they enjoyed the views of the lively harbor along with the exceptional food.

"Oh, my God, I'm stuffed," Trish said, pushing her dessert plate away. "All I'll be capable of doing this afternoon is passing out on a chaise longue on the beach."

"Me, too," Julia said, dabbing her lips with her napkin. "But this was lovely. I've never tasted a richer, more delicious sauce than the one on the Coquilles St. Jacques." She squeezed her husband's arm. "Sorry, sweetie, but I'm going to dream about it tonight."

Cameron chuckled, then took a bite of the tarte tatin they were sharing. "How in the world did a chef with so much talent for haute cuisine wind up in this tiny place?"

"He's the son of a local family," Logan said. "Studied in France at several three-star-rated restaurants, then came home to marry his childhood sweetheart."

"She's our waitress," Aidan added with a grin.

"That's so romantic," Kelly said, causing Brandon to smile as he took her hand and kissed it.

As he watched his cousins flirt with their wives, Logan had the strangest urge to drive straight back to the hotel and find Grace. He missed her and wished, not for the first time, that he'd invited her along, knowing she would fit in perfectly with his family.

"Guess there's not much chance of stealing the guy away, is there?" Adam asked, as he finished the last bite of his chocolate mousse. "We could use someone this talented at the new hotel."

"Not a chance," Aidan said firmly.

"We know," Logan chimed in, chuckling. "Because we've tried."

"What other secrets does this fabulous island hide from the rest of the world?" Kelly asked, intrigued.

"Well, since you're family," Aidan said, winking at her, "I guess it'll be okay to disclose a few secrets. For one thing, we've got amazing hot springs up in the rain forest."

"I haven't read anything about that," Kelly said, frowning.

"We've never put it in any of the brochures," Logan admitted. "Don't want anyone trampling on our own little piece of paradise."

"We won't advertise it, either," Brandon said.

"It sounds so romantic," Trish said.

"Definitely," Julia said, and gave Cameron a playful tap on his shoulder.

Cameron returned her smile, then explained, "We've got a secluded pool and a grotto on the grounds of our resort in Monarch Bay. It's pretty cool."

"And very romantic," Julia said.

"Well, our hot springs aren't quite that accessible," Aidan said, "but believe me, they're off the scale in terms of providing a romantic setting. Lush foliage, waterfalls, completely secluded."

"Oh, yeah," Logan said. "It takes some time and exercise to find them, but they're totally worth the effort once you're there."

Aidan continued describing the hike to the hot springs but Logan tuned him out. His mind had already returned instead to thoughts of Grace and the day they'd spent making love in the rain forest. He wished again that she were here with them enjoying the day and realized he hadn't yet brought her into Tierra for lunch or dinner. She would love it here, and he vowed to bring her soon.

Strange that his desire for her continued to grow instead of diminishing as he'd once thought it would. He was beginning to wonder if he would ever grow tired of her.

Logan walked into the lounge at five o'clock and was greeted by Aidan, who grabbed his arm and said without preamble, "We need to talk."

"What's up?" Logan said amiably. He was in a cheery mood, having spent the past two hours with Grace in her room. In her bed, to be more accurate. He followed Aidan to the far end of the bar, where Brandon was sitting alone, nursing a bottle of beer.

"Sit down," Aidan said to Logan, pointing to the stool next to Brandon. Then he nodded at Brandon. "Go ahead. Tell him."

Before Brandon could speak, Joey appeared in front of Logan. "What're you drinking, boss?"

"I'll have what he's having," Logan said, pointing his thumb toward the bottle in front of Brandon. "Thanks, Joey."

Aidan grabbed his own beer and stood behind the two men. "I want you to listen to Brandon."

Logan turned and eyed his brother. "I will, as soon as he says something."

Brandon swiveled his stool around and faced Logan.

"Aidan seems to think you might have a problem. So here's the deal. I want you to look across the room, over by the windows, where my mother is sitting with your father."

Logan picked out the couple in the crowd, then smiled. "Yeah, I've noticed they've been hanging out with each other, practically since the first day we all got together. You think we'll be hearing some kind of announcement pretty soon?"

"That's not the point," Aidan said sharply.

Logan whipped around. "What the hell is wrong with you?"

Brandon grinned at the two of them. "It's such a kick to see you guys together. How does anyone ever tell you apart?"

"That's not the point, either," Aidan groused.

Brandon laughed and turned back to Logan. "It's about my mom. She likes to play matchmaker."

"Are you listening?" Aidan said pointedly.

Logan ignored him. "Go on, Brandon."

Brandon nodded. "For the past half-hour, while Aidan and I have been talking here at the bar, Mom's been chatting with that pretty redheaded cocktail waitress. She's over there at the bar right now."

Logan didn't have to look to know he was talking about Grace. "Yeah, I know her," he said, his voice edged with suspicion.

"When I mentioned to Aidan that Mom had this thing about making sure everyone in her life was happily married and having babies, he thought I should warn you."

Logan turned his stool slowly around until he was facing Aidan. "You're kidding. That's what the big emergency is?"

To his credit, Aidan held up both hands in surrender. "I admit that hearing Brandon talk about it now makes it all sound a little far-fetched. But you didn't see the way Sally was talking to Grace. They were tight and it looked serious. They were making plans, I'm telling you."

"You've lost your mind," Logan muttered, shaking his head. Joey brought him his beer and Logan took a long, hard drink.

Aidan scowled. "Okay, maybe I got a little carried away in the moment."

"Maybe?"

Brandon jumped in. "Hey, I'm right there with you, Aidan. Believe me, I watched Sally take down both of my brothers and I was determined not to let it happen to me."

"But you're happily married now," Logan said in protest.

"I know." Brandon laughed. "I'll be damned if Mom didn't show up at my hotel in Napa one day, say a few words, and the next thing I knew I was walking down the aisle, happy as a clam."

"There she is," Aidan whispered loudly. "Check it out."

Logan rolled his eyes again, but turned in time to see Grace walk over to Sally's table and hand her a note. Sally stood and gave Grace a hug, then slipped the note into her small purse. Then Grace walked back to the drink station to place an order.

"Okay, that was weird," Brandon admitted.

It was, Logan had to admit. Frowning to himself, his gaze locked on Grace, he wondered what the note was all about.

"What the hell is she up to?" Logan wondered aloud.

"Thank you," Aidan said, gazing skyward, then back at his brother. "I feel slightly vindicated. I hope you're going to get to the bottom of whatever's going on."

Logan nodded, unsure of what to say or think about what he'd just seen. So, for now, he kept quiet and sipped his beer as he mulled over the possibilities and considered his next move.

Hell, it wasn't like Sally had magical powers or anything.

Oh, for God's sake. The fact that his mind had actually put those words together in a sentence meant that he had just stepped into the loony zone. Right next to his brother. The difference was, Aidan really belonged there; Logan didn't.

Contrary to Aidan's opinion, there was nothing going on between Sally and Grace. Sally was a lovely lady who took a friendly interest in all the people around her, including Grace. That was all that was going on there. Who knows, maybe Grace gave Sally her phone number so they could keep in touch. Or maybe the note held the name of some store where she liked to shop. Who the hell knew? And who cared? Besides Aidan, of course.

The real problem was that Aidan didn't trust Grace. He thought she might be after Logan's money. Logan knew it wasn't true but he hadn't done a good enough job convincing his brother. But what would be the point? This thing with Grace was temporary and he knew it. All too soon, she'd be leaving Alleria and Logan behind.

But in the meantime, Aidan had glommed on to Brandon's matchmaking conspiracy theory. Great. And Grace wasn't helping matters much since it did look like she really was going to Sally for advice. And Sally seemed happy enough to help Grace. But help her with...what? Perform a voodoo marriage chant? Sprinkle his dinner plate with aphrodisiacs? He almost laughed out loud at the thought. Grace was too down-to-earth, too literal, to buy into anything so absurd. And damn it, Sally was, too. This was all Aidan's crap and Logan needed to call him on it. Besides, the bottom line was, there was absolutely nothing that Grace—or Sally, for that matter—could do to coerce Logan into marrying her.

He would just need to do a better job of convincing Aidan of that. And then he would get off Logan's back about his relationship with Grace.

And yet, Logan had to admit that seeing Grace slip Sally that note had struck him as a little odd. But he was sure it could be easily explained. All he had to do was ask Grace about it and she would tell him the whole story. He knew Grace had a hard time lying, so it wouldn't be difficult getting the truth out of her.

But not tonight. Tonight, all he wanted to do was make love with her. Tomorrow would be soon enough to question her about Sally and the note. It was probably something completely innocent, but he knew his brother would continue tormenting him until Logan found out the truth.

Ten

"I'm going to marry her."

As Aidan's eyes widened in shock and dismay, Logan almost laughed himself silly.

"You're kidding," Aidan whispered.

"Why are you so surprised?" Logan asked. "Haven't you noticed they've been in love practically from the first day they met?"

"You noticed?" his father asked, his grin broader than Logan had ever seen it.

Logan laughed and slapped Dad on the back. "We all noticed, Dad. Except Aidan, apparently."

"Sorry, Dad. I've had a lot on my mind." Aidan scowled at Logan as he threw down the toast he'd been about to bite into. Shaking his head to rid himself of what seemed to be a pretty weird mood, Aidan pushed away from the table and walked over to Dad, who stood and wrapped him up in a bear hug.

Logan jumped up and grabbed them both fiercely. "I'm thrilled for you and Sally, Dad. She's the greatest."

"She is," Aidan said quickly. "I guess I was shocked because I never thought I'd see the day."

"Me, neither, son," Dad said, and his eyes grew misty. "But she's the woman for me. I'm in love with her and I want to be with her always. Took me long enough, but I got it right this time."

Logan felt his own eyes tear up and he willed himself to get a grip. "Where is Sally right now, Dad? I want to give her a big kiss."

"Me, too," Aidan said.

"She'll love that." Dad wiped away a happy tear. "Right now she's off making plans for us to go somewhere special for a picnic."

"Sounds great," Aidan said. "You two will have a fun day."

"But we'll celebrate tonight, right?" Logan said. "I'll reserve the table in the wine cellar and we'll all go a little crazy."

"Sounds perfect," Dad said.

Before Logan went off to find Sally, he wanted to find Grace and invite her to the family party that night. He didn't care what Aidan thought of his decision, he just wanted Grace to be with him for as long as she was on the island. He still didn't know what had gone on between her and Sally last night and while he was anxious to find out, he realized that he trusted Grace enough to know it wasn't anything sinister.

Logan turned for one last look at his dad who was still grinning from ear to ear. He hoped and prayed his father would be wearing that grin for the rest of his life. Nobody deserved happiness more than he did. When Logan thought about all the years when he and Aidan were growing up, all he could see was his father, always there. Always steady. Always loving his sons enough to make up for the loss of their mother.

Yeah, Sally Duke was perfect for Dad because Logan could see in her eyes how much she loved his father. And that made her perfect, period, as far as Logan was concerned.

The following day, the Duke brothers and their wives, along with Sally and the twins' dad, Tom, flew back to the West Coast.

"Damn, I miss them already," Aidan said as they stood together on the tarmac.

Logan agreed, staring at the sky as the jet climbed higher then curved gracefully toward the west. "Funny how we all became a family in an instant. It's like we've known them all our lives."

"I know," Aidan said. "It's comforting. A little weird, but nice."

"Really nice," Logan murmured. "Glad we got to party last night with everyone. Dad was in his element." Logan was especially glad that Grace had agreed to accompany him to the party. She'd looked beautiful and he'd been so proud to introduce her to his entire family. She'd fit in as well as he'd imagined she would.

"Yeah, it was great to see Dad and Sally together," Aidan said. "Can't wait for the wedding. It's going to be one hell of a celebration."

"Dad really deserves that."

"Yeah, he does."

Logan didn't say it out loud, but he was starting to wonder why they *all* didn't deserve that kind of happiness. Shaking his head, he said, "I was thinking…how about we build a house for Dad and Sally up on the bluff?

I know they won't live here full-time, but they might like their own place on Alleria."

"I like it. You know," Aidan said with a grin, "you're smarter than you look."

"Ah," Logan countered, with a matching grin, "twin joke. Good one."

"Okay, bro, let's get going," Aidan said, and they strolled over to the limo. Once they were settled and the driver took off, he broached the subject they'd left hanging last night. "So, did you find out about the note Grace slipped to Sally?"

"No, I didn't get a chance to ask her yet."

"Dude, you were with her all night."

"I had other things on my mind." Such as getting Grace back to his suite and into his bed. That note had been the last thing he was thinking about by then, and he smiled at the memory.

Aidan snorted. "Fine, but you'll ask her today, right?"

"Of course." Though he wasn't real anxious to open up that line of conversation and he couldn't really say why.

"Because I'll ask her myself if you don't."

"No, you won't," Logan said, jabbing his finger in the air. "Just…back off. First of all, it's probably nothing to get excited about. And second of all… Damn it, just…back off."

Aidan held his hands up in surrender. "Jeez, power down. Fine. I won't ask her. As long as you do."

"I said I would, didn't I?"

"Good. It's cool. I trust you."

"Yeah, right."

The car pulled to a stop outside the hotel entrance. Both men thanked the driver and climbed out, then Aidan checked his watch. "Look, I've got to go pack."

"Oh, hell," Logan said, rubbing his head in frustration.

"I do, too. In all of the excitement over Dad and Sally, I forgot we're leaving for New York tomorrow."

He didn't want to leave.

Logan had been dragging his ass around his bedroom, throwing socks and T-shirts into his open suitcase and counting out the required number of dress shirts and suits for the hanging bag. But the realization didn't hit him until he started pulling shoes out of the closet and lining them up next to the suitcase.

Damn. He would never disclose this to Aidan, but Logan had the strongest urge to blow off New York and stay here with Grace. They'd spent almost every night together and he was forced to admit—to himself only—that he'd grown damned close to her. He liked having her around and knew he was going to miss her while he was gone.

"Get a grip," he muttered to himself. He was only going to be gone for three days.

The problem was, he didn't know how much longer Grace intended to stay. Checking his calendar, he realized she'd been here almost three weeks. He'd never asked her how long she planned to stay. But he wanted her to be here when he got back.

If she did have to go home for a while, maybe Logan could convince her to just drop off the spores and come back right away.

"Ah, jeez." When had he turned into such a sap? Shaking his head in disgust, he stuffed his shoes into the soft cloth shoe bag, fitted them into the suitcase and zipped it closed. Nope, he definitely wouldn't be mentioning any of that to Aidan.

"What are you looking at?"

Grace jolted, startled by the voice. She hadn't heard

footsteps approaching, but that was because she tended to recede into her own little spore world when she was out here among the palms.

"I'm looking at these tiny creatures." She turned over one of the palm fronds and pointed them out to the little girl who stood a few feet away. "Can you see them?"

She took a step closer. "The little red dots?"

"That's right, although they're not actually red. More of a brownish-green. But when they're clustered together, they appear to be brick colored."

The girl frowned. "Who are you?"

"I'm Grace," she said, sitting back on her feet. "I'm a scientist and I collect these spores to use in experiments. Who are you?"

"I'm Swoozie," she said, and folded her arms across her narrow chest. "I'm staying at the hotel with my parents."

"I like your name," Grace said. "Do you like science?"

Swoozie made a face and shook her head. "I'm failing math and science."

"Oh, that's interesting. Those are my two favorite subjects." She smiled good-naturedly. "But I've always been kind of weird."

"My friend Charlotte likes math, too, but I don't get it."

Swoozie looked about ten years old, thin, with long, brown hair and big brown eyes.

"What's your favorite subject?" Grace asked as she packed up her bag.

"I guess I like English."

"Do you like to read?"

"Yes, but mostly, I just want to graduate high school so I can go and be a model in Europe."

"You want to be a model?"

"A supermodel," she specified.

"You'll need to know math and science if you're going

to be a model," Grace said casually as she stood and brushed the bits of sand and dirt off her legs.

"No, I won't."

"You will." Grace began to walk with her back to the hotel. "Say you're in Paris and you want to have dinner after your photo shoot with Pierre, the world famous French photographer. You'll need to calculate the daily exchange rate to make sure you're on budget and not overtipping your waiter. So if you know that the day's rate is 1.44 euros to the dollar, and your meal is twelve euros, you'll be able to figure out that you're about to spend over seventeen dollars, and that might not be within your budget."

"Oh." Swoozie frowned, then her face screwed up in deep thought. A few seconds later, she grinned. "But I'll be with Pierre and he'll be happy to calculate all those numbers for me."

"Well." Grace laughed and waved her hand in the air. "As long as Pierre is with you, he should just pay for your dinner."

Swoozie laughed. "That's even better."

They walked through the palmetto grove until they reached the beach. "So what are you studying in math right now?"

"Multiplication tables," Swoozie said miserably. "I'm supposed to memorize them while I'm on vacation, but I suck at memorizing stuff."

"Oh, there's a better way to learn multiplication," Grace said, leading Swoozie over to a shaded table on the terrace. "I'll show you."

Logan stood at the bar sipping his single-malt scotch as he waited for Grace to finish her shift. This would be their last night together for a few days and he didn't want to waste a minute of time, so he'd decided to camp out at the end of the bar and watch her in action until it was time for her to clock out.

She was balancing cocktail trays like a champ these days, as long as she only carried two or three drinks at a time and moved very slowly. The customers didn't seem to mind. Hell, half the time they followed her to the bar and grabbed the drinks on their own. It was a bizarre way to do business, but Logan was no longer complaining.

A thirty-something couple walked into the lounge and headed straight for the bar. The woman called the bartender over and said briskly, "Which one of your waitresses is Grace?"

Logan's hackles stiffened as he watched Sam scan the room. Spying Grace across the room wiping off a four-top for a small group of guests who waited nearby, Sam pointed her out to the couple.

"Oh, yes," the woman said, nodding. "I was told she was a redhead."

As Grace walked back toward the bar, the couple met her halfway. Logan followed them. He didn't know what this was all about, but he didn't want any trouble, especially if it involved Grace.

"So you're Grace," the woman said.

"Yes, I am," she said, smiling. "Can I help you?"

"You spoke to my daughter Swoozie this morning."

"Oh, yes. She's a sweet girl." Grace's eyes suddenly widened and she looked mortified. "Oh, I'm so sorry I suggested that Pierre pay for her dinner. I was thinking about that later and realized—"

"Thank you so much!" the woman exclaimed, and grabbed Grace in a tight embrace.

"Oh, well," Grace said, nonplussed.

"You have no idea what we've been through," Swoozie's mother cried.

The woman's husband glanced around the room nervously. When he made eye contact with Logan, he shrugged, clearly clueless.

When the mother finally let her loose, Grace raked her hair back self-consciously. "But I really didn't—"

"She came back to the room and did three pages of math homework!"

"Three pages." Grace smiled and nodded. "That's nice."

"She was so excited," the woman continued. "She kept saying 'I get it!' over and over again. When I asked her what happened, she told me you explained it to her in a way that finally clicked for her."

"I'm so glad," Grace said. "I just showed her an easy way I have of remembering number systems. I can show it to you if you'd—"

"No, no," the woman said quickly, holding up her hand as she took a step back. "Whatever you did, it worked and I'll just leave it at that. Swoozie has seen the light! That's all that matters to me. Thank you so much."

"You're welcome."

Logan stood next to Grace as the couple walked out of the bar.

"Isn't that sweet?" Grace murmured. Logan wasn't sure what had just happened, but he knew right then that Swoozie wasn't the only one Grace had helped to finally see the light.

"Come with me to the airport," Logan said early the next morning. "The driver will bring you back."

Grace was dressed in shorts, tank top and sandals, ready to leave his room. But Logan decided he didn't want to say goodbye just yet.

"Are you sure you want me there?" she asked.

"Yeah." He grabbed Grace with one hand and his suitcase with the other, and they left the suite to meet the limousine out front.

He and Grace were already waiting in the limo when Aidan climbed inside. Logan ignored his brother's fulminating glance and breathed a sigh of relief when Eleanor arrived a few seconds later. They all drove to the airport in companionable silence.

Aidan assisted Eleanor out of the car and they walked to the jet, leaving Logan to say goodbye to Grace.

Standing on the tarmac, Logan kissed her goodbye. "You'll still be here when I get back?"

"Yes, of course," Grace said with a smile. "I still have a few weeks of work to do before I have to go back to Minnesota."

"Good. I'll see you in a few days, then." He kissed her again, then turned and walked away.

"Have a good trip," Grace called.

"Hell," he muttered. A glance at the plane and his twin standing in the open doorway watching him reminded Logan that he still hadn't asked Grace about the stupid note. And if he didn't, Aidan would rag his ass for the next three days. He turned back to her. "I keep forgetting to ask you something."

"What is it?"

"You passed a note to Sally the other night in the bar. What did it say?"

She flinched and her face turned pale. "You saw that?"

"Yeah," he said, warily watching her reaction to what should've been a simple question. "What was in that note?"

Grace turned around and grabbed the limo's door handle, trying to escape. "I don't have to tell you."

"Grace," he said, reaching for her, "do you have something to hide from me?"

She glared at him. "Well, of course I do. And you have

things to hide from me. People have their secrets. It's human nature."

"What was in the note, Grace?" he asked, his tone deadly quiet.

Her jaw was set in a stubborn scowl and as much as she tried to hold to her convictions, Logan continued to stare her down. Finally, she broke, and exhaled heavily. "Fine. I gave her directions. Are you happy?"

"Directions to what?" he shouted. "Her G-spot?"

"Oh, for God's sake, Logan," she said, throwing up her hands in exasperation. "Sally doesn't need help finding her G-spot."

Oh, he so didn't need to know that about his soon-to-be new mother. "Then what? Just tell me."

She huffed and puffed and fumed, and Logan had the strongest urge to kiss her senseless. But first he needed to know the truth.

She wrapped her arms tightly around her middle. "She wanted directions to the hot springs. There, are you happy?"

Seriously? The hot springs? That was the big secret? Logan frowned at that. "Why would she want to go there?"

"You're kidding, right?" Grace rolled her eyes, then slapped her hands on her hips and said, "She wanted to take your father there, but she didn't want anyone else to know that they were sneaking off to have wild jungle sex."

"Oh, no, no, no." Logan stumbled back a half step, pretty certain that his own face had grown pale, too. Grace had just painted a picture in his mind that he would've been perfectly happy never to have seen in his entire life.

And if not for Aidan bugging him to find out, he never would have. It would be his pleasure to share that horrifying mental image with his twin.

"And don't you dare tell her I told you," Grace said, her voice stinging with aggravation.

"I won't, don't worry. In fact, I'm going to do everything I can to forget you ever told me." He stared at her for another ten seconds, then began to chuckle. "Jesus, Grace." He laughed out loud, then yanked her close and planted a hot, wet kiss on her lips. "God, I'm going to miss you."

She pressed her palm against his chest. "I'll miss you, too, Logan."

He gave her one more hard, fast kiss, then turned and jogged to the plane. Still laughing, he climbed the stairs, then spun around and waved goodbye one last time.

Eleven

Grace was a pathetic mess. She missed Logan terribly, and he'd only been gone one day. What in the world would she do once she was back home in Minnesota? Once she left Alleria, she would never see Logan again. So wasn't it about time she pulled herself together and figured out the best way to deal with the pain?

But a long, sleepless night wasn't the way to get used to anything. Every time she closed her eyes, she saw Logan. A tight ball of misery lodged in the pit of her stomach, reminding her with every breath that this was just the beginning. That leaving Logan would be the hardest thing she had ever done.

By morning, she was exhausted and feeling sorry for herself, so she spent several hours in the rain forest, hiking and searching for more spore sites. But even her research couldn't fill the void that was building inside her. That evening, she worked tirelessly in the cocktail lounge and even stayed an extra hour later to help the others.

She loved the camaraderie among the waiters and bartenders and busboys. Sometimes she wished she could just go and be a waitress because the people were so much more fun than academics. Sad but true.

But even though she wished she could stay on the island forever, she knew she needed to get back to the laboratory. She had important work to do there. Besides, this wasn't her world. Was it? She'd lived her entire life in academia. Could she honestly leave it all behind? Could she really see herself living here in paradise?

"Oh, dear," she whispered, and tried to swallow around the sudden lump in her throat as she watched Dee laugh at something Joey said. She thought of Logan and all the nights he'd stood at the end of the bar waiting for her. And that's when it struck her that she really could live here forever. And the realization scared her to death.

Working all these long hours had done little to take her mind off missing Logan. It didn't help that tonight everyone was talking about the possibility of a tropical storm off the coast of South America turning into a hurricane as it headed north toward Alleria. She didn't want to be in a hurricane without Logan.

The very notion of riding out a hurricane was terrifying to her, but some of the staff were taking it in stride. They had experienced severe storms and hurricanes in the past and were confident that Logan's hotel was so well built that it could withstand the worst that Mother Nature could throw at it.

As Grace returned to the bar for another drink order, she noticed it had grown breezier in the lounge. The manager asked some of the men to close the casement windows along the outer perimeter of the room so the guests would be more comfortable.

"It's so chilly tonight," Dee said, rubbing her arms as they waited together at the bar for their orders. "And I've got a jacket on."

"I wish I had my sweater," Grace said after noticing that several of the waitresses were covered up. Dee's denim jacket looked cute over her sarong.

"Why don't you run and get it?" Dee said. "I'll watch your tables for a few minutes."

"Are you sure?"

"Absolutely. If you're sticking around to help us, we don't want you freezing to death."

"Okay, I'll hurry back."

"No worries."

Grace left the bar and started walking back to her room, but remembered she'd left her pink sweater in Logan's suite the other night. He'd recently given her a copy of his key card to use when she worked late, so she hurried over to his side of the hotel and used the card to slip inside.

She switched on the light, glanced around the room and saw her sweater on the chair near his desk. She grabbed it, then noticed the thick set of architectural drawings spread out on his desk.

Her curiosity was piqued and she rounded the desk to see what they were. Grace had never seen blueprints before and appreciated the architectural precision of the lines and angles. She smiled as she realized that these were the plans for the sports center Logan and his brother were going to build. He was excited about creating a destination for sports enthusiasts here on Alleria and had described it in detail. That was the reason he'd gone to New York, to meet with the investors and finalize these plans.

Studying the blueprints made her feel closer to Logan somehow. She knew he had studied the same drawings and probably pictured the finished creation in his mind. She tried to do that as she gazed at all the little side drawings and various site descriptions.

And that's when she saw it: the map and description of the location of the gigantic sports complex in relationship to the hotel. North side. Adjacent. Palmetto grove.

"No," she whispered.

She walked around the desk, certain at first that she was interpreting the drawings all wrong. But she wasn't a dummy, and after ten minutes of studying every sheet in the stack, she knew she had been betrayed. He had lied to her. Okay, he hadn't lied exactly, but he'd clearly avoided telling her the truth as he let her gather her spores and talk about the importance of her research, all the while knowing that he planned to pave over the whole site.

Logan and his brother had every intention of building their sports center directly on top of the land where the spores grew.

She backed away from the desk. Maybe there was some mistake. But she knew there wasn't. So why hadn't Logan said something to her? He knew how important her research was. Had he simply been using sex as a way of distracting her from his plans for eradicating the very spores she'd come there to study?

Or maybe he'd simply been carrying out what he'd promised her from the very beginning. He'd wanted her off the island and he would do whatever it took to get rid of her.

Oh, but that was ridiculous. This wasn't personal. It wasn't about her. It wasn't about her spores. It was just the way businessmen conducted business. Destroy a few billion spores to build a few tennis courts? Sure, if that's what made money. Never mind the possibility of curing disease and saving lives.

"Oh, God." Not only would this plan eviscerate the spores but it would destroy the foundation of her life's work. Her funding would dry up and there would be no possibility of continuing her research.

"Stop," she cried. She needed to calm down and think instead of going crazy. Of course there would still be spores. Logan wouldn't destroy the entire rain forest, for goodness' sake. But the fact remained that he knew how important it was to Grace that the palm trees and their spores be kept safe and intact. And he'd blithely decided to destroy a large swath of it.

"How could he do it?" she mumbled over and over. And how could she have trusted him? That question was more easily answered than the first. She was simply a dim-witted woman who'd fallen in love with a man who didn't respect her or her life or her goals.

With a sharp cry, she ran from Logan's suite and headed for her own. Friends smiled and tried to talk to her as she passed, but Grace hardly saw them. Her mind was churning, her vision blurry with unshed tears and her heart was heavy with a pain she wasn't sure she could survive.

She ran inside her room and slammed the door shut. Then she crawled onto the bed, shivering in humiliation.

She might've lain there for a few minutes or a few hours, she would never be sure. Finally, she stumbled across the room and fumbled in her purse for her cell phone. Stabbing the buttons, she called her friend and mentor, Phillippa, and prayed that she would pick up before it went to voice mail.

"Grace, is that you? It's so late. What's going on?"

Grace quickly explained the situation and was gratified when Phillippa blurted an expletive.

"Why, that lousy spore killer," she said stoutly, and Grace could picture Phillippa's glasses sliding down her nose. "How could he do this to you? Were you aware that he was so environmentally unfriendly?"

Maybe he was, but despite everything, Grace couldn't bear to hear any criticism of Logan. She just wanted to save the spores. "Do you know how to stop him?"

"Oh, yeah," Phillippa said. "It's called an injunctive order and we're going to slap it on him so hard, he won't know what hit him."

Before she hung up, Phillippa took a minute to warn Grace that Walter's funding had come through. Grace slid down onto the chair, unable to speak. Yes, she would go back and face the grant committee and tell them how he had lied. And she would present them with her own latest findings based on her new collection of super spores. But still, how could the committee have fallen for Walter's lies? How could they have awarded him one cent?

It was a double blow. Now she'd been betrayed on two fronts. She could care less about Walter, but she hated to go back to the university and face all those sympathetic stares. But that would be a piece of cake compared to the way she would feel if she stayed on the island. There was no way she could face Logan after finding out he'd been playing her for a fool all this time. Walter's lies were nothing compared to Logan's betrayal. She'd thought he was different and it hurt to know how very wrong she'd been. So much for all that intelligence she was so famous for.

With a bitter sigh, she pulled her bags out of the closet and began to pack. It was difficult because her eyes were blurry from the tears she didn't seem able to stop.

There was a knock on the door.

For one second she thought it might be Logan. Then her brain cleared. He was still in New York arranging for the money to kill her career. That would take him another day or two at least. Without even realizing it, anger began to film over some of her pain as she hurried to the door and opened it.

"Oh, Dee," she cried. "I'm so sorry."

"Gracie, you never came back to—" Dee stopped and glanced around the room.

Grace realized it looked like the hurricane had already struck. "I'm packing. I need to go home."

"What's going on?"

"Nothing," she said, then realized how absurd that sounded, even to her. Sitting down on the edge of the bed, she told Dee the whole story.

"It just doesn't sound like Logan," Dee murmured, shaking her head.

"I didn't think so, either," Grace said miserably. "But I saw the plans myself, Dee. There's no mistake."

Dee pulled her close for a hug. "I hate that you're leaving, Gracie, but I understand. It's no more than he deserves, the lying rat-dog. I'm sorry he hurt you."

"Me, too."

"Will you call?" Dee asked, standing up and stepping back. "Let me know you're okay? I mean, just because you're leaving doesn't mean we can't still be friends, right?"

One bright spot in a completely hideous day, Grace thought, and hugged Dee fiercely. "Thank you! I will call. I promise."

After Dee left, Grace continued packing. When she was finished, she called the concierge to ask about flights. That brought on another dismal round of tears. She'd grown to love it here. She loved her friends and her job and the palm trees and the rain forest and the beach and her poor little spores.

And she loved Logan.

In spite of what he'd done, she'd fallen in love with him. And while that meant she had to be the biggest twit in the universe, she loved him and knew she always would. And the fact that he was never going to be hers brought another sharp pain to her chest.

She spent a long night staring out the window at the ebbing storm, and early the next morning, Grace left a polite note for Logan with the concierge, then took the first flight off the island.

The jet reached cruising altitude and Logan stretched his legs out on the seat facing him. The meetings were over, the investors' checks were deposited, and the Alleria sports center would soon be a reality. Eleanor walked into the cabin and handed Logan and Aidan each a glass of champagne.

"Thanks, Ellie."

The mood was festive as they toasted to their success and drank down the cold, bubbly liquid.

"That's good," Aidan murmured, grinning. "We did good."

"Yeah, we did good," Logan said.

Ellie giggled. "Life is good."

They all laughed, then Logan said, "Man, I can't wait to see Grace."

"What?" Aidan twisted around to stare at him.

"Aww," Ellie said, and smiled warmly at him.

Logan frowned. "Did I say that out loud?"

"Yeah, you did."

He glanced from Ellie to Aidan. "Huh."

"Ah, hell," Aidan said in disgust. "Now you've done it."

"Done what?"

"You've gone and fallen in love with her."

"Don't be—" He started to protest automatically, then stopped. And thought about it. Hard.

Love. Just saying the word in his head didn't strike the same raw nerve it had in the past. Did that mean it was true? Was he in love with Grace? The idea didn't rankle him as it had in the past. In fact, it made him smile.

Ever since he'd talked to Brandon out on the beach, Logan had been thinking about things. The past. The future. Love and life. Risk. Trust.

He'd spent half of his life fearing to trust in love. He'd talked himself into marrying Tanya, thinking he should give love a try. But he'd never loved her. The fact that she'd cheated on him was as good an excuse as any to never try again.

But these few days away from Grace had made him realize how much he wanted to try. The thing was, his world felt empty without her. He couldn't wait to get home to see her. He wanted to know how she'd spent her days, wanted to hear what was new with the spores.

It was staggering to realize that he'd actually fallen in love for the first and last time in his life.

He tested the words over and over again in his mind and when he was certain that he wasn't going to be struck by lightning, he decided to say them aloud.

"I'm in love with her."

Aidan buried his head in his hands.

As they climbed down the stairs and stepped onto the tarmac, Aidan slung his arm around Logan's shoulder and said, "Wonder if Dad and Sally are in some hot tub in San Francisco right now...how did Gracie put it? 'Having hot jungle sex'?"

"Oh, man." Logan slapped his hands over his ears and started humming loudly.

Aidan laughed uproariously, then calmed down and admitted, "Okay, I'm going to say something I never thought I would. I like her, bro."

"Good," Logan said, knowing he was talking about Grace. "Because I'm in love with the confounded woman and that's all there is to it."

"If you had to take the fall, she was a good one to pick. So if it matters to you, you've got my blessing."

"It matters," Logan admitted, glancing at his twin. "Thank you."

Aidan grinned. "Let's go tell her the good news."

The brothers strolled across the lobby wheeling their luggage behind them.

"Oh, Mr. Sutherland," Harrison, the concierge, called out. "I have a letter for you." He pulled an envelope from his desk and rushed over to the twins.

Aidan took it, glanced at the envelope and handed it to Logan. "It's for you."

Logan stared at his name on the envelope. He might've waited to open it when he was alone, but something niggled at him and he opened it right there. A minute later, he let the note drop to the floor.

Aidan picked it up and read the words. "She left? She just left? What did you do to her?"

Logan shook his head, too dumbfounded to answer.

"Come on," Aidan said, pushing him forward. "We'll go to your room and call her."

They made it to Logan's room, but before they could get inside, Dee came running up the hall. "There you are! Why did you do it?"

Logan scowled at her. "Close the damn door."

Aidan pulled her inside and led her over to the chair in front of Logan's desk. "Sit. Talk. Tell us what you know."

"I don't care if you're my boss. What you—he—you—" she looked from one to the other of them. "What Logan did to Gracie was just plain mean and underhanded and—"

"What did Grace say?" Aidan demanded since Logan was staring into space.

"He knows what he did," Dee said, pointing at Logan. Then she pointed at Aidan. "For Pete's sake, which one of you is which?"

"I'm Aidan," he said. "Now tell us everything that happened."

Logan sat behind his desk with his elbows resting on the surface and listened to Dee's story.

When she was finished, Aidan scratched his head. "What the hell?"

"We're not killing any spores," Logan muttered.

"That's what she said," Dee insisted, then shook her head in confusion. "She left the bar to get her sweater and the next thing I knew, she was in her room crying her eyes out about you paving over the rain forest."

"It was her pink sweater," Logan murmured. "I remember seeing it and meant to bring it to her."

"Right," Dee said. "She came in here to get her sweater and all hell broke loose. It wasn't enough for that creep Walter to break her heart, but then you had to come along and—"

"Who the hell is Walter?" Logan said, his voice belonging more to a growling animal than a normal human.

Dee told them the whole ugly story of Walter's betrayal and how much it had messed up Grace's life. Then Dee took off, leaving the men to brood on their own.

Logan stared at his desk for a long time, until he realized it wasn't his desk he was seeing but the thick pack of old blueprints he'd left spread out here. The new ones were on his desk in the corporate office down the hall. "Oh, crap."

"What?" Aidan said.

"She saw the old plans," he said, tapping the blueprints.

Aidan got closer and peered at them. "Those are two years old."

"I know. They're completely obsolete. But she must've seen them and jumped to the conclusion that I was going to pour cement over the freaking palmetto grove."

"She thought you betrayed her."

Aidan frowned as he beat the edge of the desk with his knuckles. "Now we know why she left in such a hurry."

"Damn it," Logan said, letting loose a sigh loaded with frustration.

"Look, just call her and tell her she's wrong."

"Hell, no," Logan said, his eyes focused on the blue site map in the corner of the wide sheet. "She didn't even trust me enough to ask me about any of this. She just assumed the worst and took off. Who's betraying whom?"

There was a knock on the door.

"Now what?" Aidan said. He opened the door and a guy slapped a blue-backed form at him.

"What is this?"

"Injunction," the guy said. "You've been served."

Logan prowled his office like a caged animal. It had been three days since Grace had left, three days that he'd spent chastising himself for falling for a woman who was willing to leave him without a word. Grace had walked out on him as easily as the mother he barely remembered. As easily as his cheating wife had driven away from him that night four years ago.

So much for love. *Love.* He laughed without humor. What a great cosmic joke. Hopefully this was the last lesson needed to prove to him that love simply didn't exist. Not for him. Ever.

As he paced around his desk for the tenth time, he saw the injunction sitting there and his anger festered all over again. He stared at the new blueprints and the contracts stacked on the conference table, then back at the original site map that had caused all the trouble in the first place.

And a plan began to form in his mind.

Grace was miserable and utterly confused. Always in the past, she'd been able to count on science to clear up any questions for her. But what she still felt for Logan simply wasn't logical. If this was love, why did it have to hurt so much?

She had tried to bury herself in university life again but she found that world was no longer a good fit. Heck, maybe it never had been, only she hadn't had a choice. Now, all she could do was remember Alleria and how she'd spent her days working and her nights loving Logan.

Still, that part of her life was over and so she'd applied for funding and was waiting to hear back. It had warmed her heart to hear that Phillippa and two department heads had written to protest Walter's funding, threatening legal action. Phillippa promised that as long as she had breath in her body, Walter wouldn't get away with stealing Grace's work. Knowing Phillippa, Grace was sure it was only a matter of time before Walter was dragged into court with his tail between his legs. A good thing, because now more than ever, Grace needed her research funding. It was all she had left.

She forced herself to work. It was the one thing that had been there for her throughout her life. And now that she'd lost Logan, work was especially important.

But then, she hadn't really lost Logan, had she? How

could she, when he'd never been hers to begin with? And that line of thinking just made her hurt all over again, so she stared into the eyepiece of the electron microscope and lost herself in the world of spores.

In the background, she heard the door open, followed by several sets of footsteps. It was probably Phillippa and some other lab tech. Whoever it was, she wasn't interested in talking to them. She just wanted everyone to leave her alone to find her way back to some sense of normalcy.

Grace continued to stare at the slide in front of her, marveling at the pace of replication the new spores were exhibiting.

"She's right over there," Phillippa said.

"Yes, I see her," a man said.

Chills skittered across Grace's shoulders at the sound of that voice. She pulled away from the microscope and turned in time to see Phillippa step out of the room and close the door behind her.

"Logan?"

"How are you, Grace?"

"I'm…" What was she? Not fine, certainly. Lonely? Miserable? Unhappy? In love?

He didn't seem to need an answer, just walked over and handed her a folded document. "This is for you."

She stared at the papers in her hand, then back at him. He looked wonderful, although his eyes and mouth showed signs of strain. It didn't matter. He was still the most handsome man she'd ever seen. And the only man she'd ever loved. Tears swam in her eyes, blurring her vision. She whipped around so he wouldn't see her swipe her hand to brush away the tears.

"What is it?" she asked numbly.

"It's a deed to the palmetto grove and that hillside in the rain forest where the wild palms grow. If you'd stuck around a few more days, I could've given it to you before you left."

Her hand fisted on the papers and she gawked at him. "What? Why? Why would you do this?"

"Why?" He folded his arms across his chest. "Because now you'll always know for sure that the spores are safe."

"They're safe?"

He shook his head in annoyance. "Damn it, Grace, you served me with an injunction against building anything on that land in perpetuity. So yeah, they're safe. What I don't understand is why you felt like you had to have sex with me to save the damn spores. You could've just asked me."

She gasped. "I didn't have sex with you to save the—"

"You didn't trust me, Grace. Don't you know I would never destroy anything that was so important to you?"

"I didn't—"

"Look, Grace. To be honest, it was never about you or the spores anyway. We moved the site of the sports center two years ago."

She frowned at him. "But I saw the plans."

"You saw an old set of blueprints that I was just looking at for reference. So next time you're snooping, check the dates."

"You were never going to build near the spores?"

Logan studied her for a long moment, his face unreadable. "No."

She exhaled heavily. "I thought…"

"You assumed I was such a jerk that I would unceremoniously tear up the rain forest and destroy the entire ecosystem of the island just to build a few tennis courts. That makes me sound like a pretty big jackass, all right. No wonder you took off."

"I—I thought…"

"You thought I was too stupid to understand what it meant to you."

"No. I've never thought you were stupid." She groped for the words. "I just thought you didn't care."

"I cared," he said tightly. "It was you who didn't care. It was you who didn't trust."

She tried to blink back the tears but it was too late. Her cheeks were wet with them. "Logan, I'm so sorry. I didn't think you cared about my research."

"I care about *you,* Grace. You should've trusted me." He came up close and tapped the deed in her hand. "There are your damn spores. You got what you wanted."

He turned to leave.

"I wanted you," she whispered.

He turned back around and laughed shortly. "You're way too smart for that."

Then he left.

The room was silent except for the sound of Grace's heart shattering. Grabbing a fistful of tissues, she collapsed onto her lab stool and buried her head in her arms.

She didn't know if a body could survive this much heartache. And the fact that she'd inflicted so much pain on Logan made her pain even worse. She wanted to crawl into a hole and hide, she felt so awful. Could her crippled heart withstand this much agony?

A minute later, she felt a hand on her back.

"Logan?"

"It's me, Grace," Phillippa said. "I eavesdropped through the door. I'm so sorry."

"Oh, God, I'm an idiot," she wailed.

Phillippa grimaced. "Yeah, I kind of think that might be true."

Grace looked up through her tears. "Whose side are you on?"

"Sorry, honey." Phillippa patted her back again. "But wow, that guy must really love you to give up that land for you. And to come all this way just to tell you so? How do you feel about him?"

Sniffling, Grace rubbed her stomach. "I feel sick and dizzy and clueless and stupid. My heart aches and my throat feels like there's a boulder stuck in there. It's hard to swallow. Everything hurts and I can barely stand up, I feel so miserable."

"Ah," Phillippa said, nudging her glasses up her nose. "Sounds like you're in love with him, too. I would say you're probably going to have to do a lot of groveling to get him back."

Back on the island, Logan was making everyone crazy. He would complain to anyone who was willing to listen that he felt used, abandoned and betrayed. And since he was the boss, everyone felt compelled to listen.

He grumbled to Aidan about how pissed off he was that once again, he'd trusted the wrong woman and he would never risk his heart again.

He didn't mention to a living soul that he missed Grace more than he would have ever thought possible. The days were miserable, but the nights without her were torture. He couldn't sleep. Couldn't eat. Hell, he couldn't even enjoy a damn walk on his own damn island because he kept *seeing* her there.

Aidan popped open two beers and handed one to Logan.

"Thanks," Logan muttered, and took a big gulp.

Aidan sat down in the chair across from him. "Dude, you've gotta stop bitching and moaning to the staff. You're starting to sound like a girl and I think you're scaring the housekeepers."

"Tough," Logan said.

Aidan didn't speak for a time and they both drank their beers in peace and quiet. But it couldn't last.

"You know," Aidan said, "you once told me that part of Grace's charm was that she didn't expect anything from you."

Logan's eyes narrowed on his brother. "I never said that."

"Yeah, you did," Aidan said. "But listen, there's nothing charming about having low expectations. It's heartbreaking, is what it is. Grace obviously learned the hard way to lower her expectations when it comes to a man having feelings for her."

"Since when did you become a philosopher?"

Aidan spoke through clenched teeth. "I'm just trying to help you out here, bro. It's painful to see you acting like such a jerk."

"Look," Logan said, "I made a mistake falling for Grace and I'm determined to put that mistake behind me. It might take a little time so I would appreciate some damn patience from my twin."

"Time isn't gonna help you, Logan," Aidan told him solemnly.

Logan didn't believe it. He would conquer this. Any day now.

But he continued to walk around in a fury for the next few days until Aidan and most of the staff were no longer talking to him.

The phone rang and Logan punched the speaker button. "What is it?"

"We've got a situation in the cocktail lounge," Aidan said. "Get out here now."

Logan shook his head in irritation. Why couldn't anyone handle anything around here without him? Muttering an expletive, he pushed away from the desk and took off down the hall.

As he came within a few yards of the doorway into the lounge, the strident sound of breaking glass resounded from inside the bar.

"What the hell?" Logan groused, and walked into the large, open room. The first and only thing he saw was Grace in an impossibly sexy bikini and see-through sarong. She stood a few feet away, staring down at a pile of broken glass and liquid oozing across the sleek wood floor.

"Oops," she said.

"Hello, Grace," he said.

She looked up. "Oh, hello, Logan."

"You're fired." He turned to leave before he did something stupid like sweep her up against him and kiss her until neither of them could breathe. He'd already learned that sex wasn't the answer, though he wanted her more than ever. The fact that she was here didn't mean a damn thing had changed.

"You can't fire me."

He whirled around. "Oh, yeah? Why not?"

"Because I love you."

Logan glared at her in spite of the fact that his heart took a hard lurch at her words. "Oh, really? I thought you were way too smart to fall for someone like me."

She smiled. "As it turns out, I'm a complete idiot."

He sighed. "No you're not, Grace."

"It's true." She walked up close to him and pressed her hand against his chest.

He was helpless to move. Damn it, he didn't *want* to move. Just her touch was enough to ease away the pain of the past few days. "Grace."

"It's no excuse for the way I behaved," she said, "but

I've grown used to men walking away from me in my life. I just assumed you would do it, too."

"You didn't trust me."

"I did, Logan. I trusted you with my heart."

"But not with your spores." Logan wondered if this conversation sounded as weird to everyone else in the room as it sounded to him. It didn't matter. He wanted to get it over with. "Grace, you didn't trust me enough to do the right thing."

"I know and I'll never forgive myself. I was wrong. I admit it. Can you ever forgive me and let me back into your life?"

"I'm not sure."

"Oh, for God's sake," Aidan shouted in exasperation from across the room. "Just kiss the girl and get on with it."

Logan pierced him with a look. "You of all people should understand why trust is so important."

"Yeah, yeah, your ex-wife cheated," Aidan said, shaking his head. "Blah, blah, blah."

Logan bared his teeth and Grace gasped, but Aidan ignored it all. "And not only was she a cheat, but thanks to the Switch, we found out she was too self-involved to take the time to learn the differences between you and me."

"What's your point, Aidan?" Logan said.

"My point is that Grace could see the differences from the first minute she met me. That's because Grace is in love with you. Even I figured that out. And I think she's earned your forgiveness. Haven't you, Grace?"

Grace flashed Aidan a sweet smile that pissed off Logan even more.

"Logan," Grace said, forcing his attention back to her. "It never occurred to me that you would care. Nobody's ever cared, so I didn't know what that looked like or felt like. I should've, but I didn't. And that makes me as stupid—"

"You're not stupid."

"Yes," she said earnestly. "I'm as stupid as a big bag of dirt."

Logan was taken aback. "That's a little harsh, Grace."

"It true, a big bag of dirt, with sphagnum and peat moss thrown in there."

"Sounds like potting soil."

She clapped her hands. "See how smart you are? No wonder I love you so much."

Logan laughed and pulled her into his arms. "So are you, because you came back to me."

"Kiss me, please?"

He kissed her. "I love you, Grace."

"Oh, Logan, I love you, too." She stretched up on her toes and met his mouth in a kiss meant to seal a promise.

Logan touched her cheek. "But you're still fired, Grace. I can't afford the breakage bills."

"Fine," she said, laughing. "But I'm not leaving here, ever again."

"What about your laboratory?"

"I don't care," she said. "I'll...well, to be honest, I don't know what I'll do. But I'm not worried."

"I'm not worried, either," he said, wrapping his arms around her. "Because I'm going to find a nice spot to break ground on a new research lab right here on the island."

She gazed up at him. "You'd build a lab for me?"

Logan saw a sheen of tears in her eyes and his heart overflowed with joy for this very smart woman who'd stolen his heart. "I'd do just about anything for you, Grace. If you hadn't come back to me, I would've gone to get you in another day or two. I can't live without you, spores and all."

Applause broke out in the bar as Logan and Grace sealed their love with another long kiss and a whispered promise to each other that they would always be together.

* * * * *

PASSION

For a spicier, decidedly hotter read—
this is your destination for romance!

COMING NEXT MONTH
AVAILABLE JANUARY 10, 2012

#2131 TERMS OF ENGAGEMENT
Ann Major

#2132 SEX, LIES AND THE SOUTHERN BELLE
Dynasties: The Kincaids
Kathie DeNosky

#2133 THE NANNY BOMBSHELL
Billionaires and Babies
Michelle Celmer

#2134 A COWBOY COMES HOME
Colorado Cattle Barons
Barbara Dunlop

#2135 INTO HIS PRIVATE DOMAIN
The Men of Wolff Mountain
Janice Maynard

#2136 A SECRET BIRTHRIGHT
Olivia Gates

You can find more information on upcoming Harlequin® titles,
free excerpts and more at www.HarlequinInsideRomance.com.

HDCNM1211

REQUEST YOUR FREE BOOKS!
2 FREE NOVELS PLUS 2 FREE GIFTS!

Harlequin® *Desire*

ALWAYS POWERFUL, PASSIONATE AND PROVOCATIVE

YES! Please send me 2 FREE Harlequin Desire® novels and my 2 FREE gifts (gifts are worth about $10). After receiving them, if I don't wish to receive any more books, I can return the shipping statement marked "cancel." If I don't cancel, I will receive 6 brand-new novels every month and be billed just $4.30 per book in the U.S. or $4.99 per book in Canada. That's a saving of at least 14% off the cover price! It's quite a bargain! Shipping and handling is just 50¢ per book in the U.S. and 75¢ per book in Canada.* I understand that accepting the 2 free books and gifts places me under no obligation to buy anything. I can always return a shipment and cancel at any time. Even if I never buy another book, the two free books and gifts are mine to keep forever.

225/326 HDN FEF3

Name _____ (PLEASE PRINT)

Address _____ Apt. #

City _____ State/Prov. _____ Zip/Postal Code

Signature (if under 18, a parent or guardian must sign)

Mail to the **Reader Service:**
IN U.S.A.: P.O. Box 1867, Buffalo, NY 14240-1867
IN CANADA: P.O. Box 609, Fort Erie, Ontario L2A 5X3

Not valid for current subscribers to Harlequin Desire books.

Want to try two free books from another line?
Call 1-800-873-8635 or visit www.ReaderService.com.

* Terms and prices subject to change without notice. Prices do not include applicable taxes. Sales tax applicable in N.Y. Canadian residents will be charged applicable taxes. Offer not valid in Quebec. This offer is limited to one order per household. All orders subject to credit approval. Credit or debit balances in a customer's account(s) may be offset by any other outstanding balance owed by or to the customer. Please allow 4 to 6 weeks for delivery. Offer available while quantities last.

Your Privacy—The Reader Service is committed to protecting your privacy. Our Privacy Policy is available online at www.ReaderService.com or upon request from the Reader Service.

We make a portion of our mailing list available to reputable third parties that offer products we believe may interest you. If you prefer that we not exchange your name with third parties, or if you wish to clarify or modify your communication preferences, please visit us at www.ReaderService.com/consumerchoice or write to us at Reader Service Preference Service, P.O. Box 9062, Buffalo, NY 14269. Include your complete name and address.

HDES11B

Harlequin *Presents*

USA TODAY bestselling author

Penny Jordan

brings you her newest romance

PASSION AND THE PRINCE

Prince Marco di Lucchesi can't hide his proud disdain for fiery English rose Lily Wrightington—or his attraction to her! While touring the palazzos of northern Italy, the atmosphere heats up...until shadows from Lily's past come out....

Can Marco keep his passion under wraps enough to protect her, or will it unleash itself, too?

Find out in January 2012!

*Brittany Grayson survived a horrible ordeal at the hands
of a serial killer known as The Professional…
who's after her now?*

*Harlequin® Romantic Suspense presents a new installment
in Carla Cassidy's reader-favorite miniseries,*
LAWMEN OF BLACK ROCK.

Enjoy a sneak peek of
TOOL BELT DEFENDER.

*Available January 2012
from Harlequin® Romantic Suspense.*

"**B**rittany?" His voice was deep and pleasant and made
her realize she'd been staring at him openmouthed through
the screen door.

"Yes, I'm Brittany and you must be…" Her mind suddenly went blank.

"Alex. Alex Crawford, Chad's friend. You called him
about a deck?"

As she unlocked the screen, she realized she wasn't
quite ready yet to allow a stranger inside, especially a male
stranger.

"Yes, I did. It's nice to meet you, Alex. Let's walk around
back and I'll show you what I have in mind," she said. She
frowned as she realized there was no car in her driveway.
"Did you walk here?" she asked.

His eyes were a warm blue that stood out against his
tanned face and was complemented by his slightly shaggy
dark hair. "I live three doors up." He pointed up the street to
the Walker home that had been on the market for a while.

"How long have you lived there?"

"I moved in about six weeks ago," he replied as they

walked around the side of the house.

That explained why she didn't know the Walkers had moved out and Mr. Hard Body had moved in. Six weeks ago she'd still been living at her brother Benjamin's house trying to heal from the trauma she'd lived through.

As they reached the backyard she motioned toward the broken brick patio just outside the back door. "What I'd like is a wooden deck big enough to hold a barbecue pit and an umbrella table and, of course, lots of people."

He nodded and pulled a tape measure from his tool belt. "An outdoor entertainment area," he said.

"Exactly," she replied and watched as he began to walk the site. The last thing Brittany had wanted to think about over the past eight months of her life was men. But looking at Alex Crawford definitely gave her a slight flutter of pure feminine pleasure.

*Will Brittany be able to heal in the arms of Alex,
her hotter-than-sin handyman...or will a second
psychopath silence her forever? Find out in*
TOOL BELT DEFENDER
*Available January 2012
from Harlequin® Romantic Suspense
wherever books are sold.*